FOREWORD

I guess I know a little something about zombies needing love, considering I made a cheap independent zombie movie called *The Stink of Flesh* wherein a fellow keeps a nude female zombie chained in the tool shed ("I didn't see *that* coming," my buddy Don Adams said when we were watching the movie in his Hollywood apartment), eventually visiting her for a little of the old gorilla-in-the-washing-machine when things get hairy with the wife. If you know what I mean.

And yet, I have no love for the living dead.

Oh, don't get me wrong—I freaking *love* zombies, been nuts about 'em ever since I was 10 years old and saw the original *Night of the Living Dead* on *Creepy Creature Feature* one Saturday night. That little event screwed up my ability to sleep for quite some time afterwards, I can assure you. And I've gone out of my way to see every zombie movie I could get my hands on ever since—a high point being a showing of Lucio Fulci's *Zombie* at the drive-in in Flatwoods, Kentucky (where we went in Billy Ray Cyrus's dad's car) and some chubby ol' redneck gal threw up during the hunk-of-wood-in-the-eye scene.

But if my best girl came wandering into the room, drooling and growling, her flesh beginning to decompose, her teeth gnashing as she mindlessly eyeballed my delicious flesh? I'd put a round right between my sweet baby's eyes.

In this book, however, you'll find folks—living and undead—who feel differently about the whole scenario. And some of them get more than a little carried away.

I don't personally know any of the authors who contributed their fine stories to this volume, and being an author myself, I know better than to confuse the writer with the writing. But sometimes, I kinda have to stop and go *what in the holy hell . . . ?*

But like I say: don't confuse the writer with the writing. I certainly don't wanna bang a dead chick in a tool shed.

Unless there's some way to bring something similar to the 3-second rule into the mix. A little warmth left in the corpse, know what I'm sayin'?

Wait. Forget I said anything.

Just read the book. Make up your own mind. But when it comes to sex and death?

I'll take the sex. You can keep the death.

Scott S. Phillips
Writer and director of *THE STINK OF FLESH*
October 8, 2012

ZOMBIES
need love, too

edited by
MAX BOOTH III

illustrations by
APRIL GUADIANA

introduction by
SCOTT S. PHILLIPS

Dark Moon Books

DARK MOON BOOKS
Largo, Florida

ZOMBIES NEED LOVE TOO...

ISBN: 978-0-9885569-6-6

Dark Moon Books
An imprint of Stony Meadow Publishing
3412 Imperial Palm Drive
Largo, FL 33771
Visit our website at www.darkmoonbooks.com

Printed in the United States of America

Cover Artwork: April Guadiana

CONTENTS

UNDER MY SKIN

ARAMINTA STAR MATTHEWS

I RECOGNIZED HER tonight by her fingers.

Long, white bones wrapped in stretched-white skin—a piano player's fingers—clutching the edge of the door to her brownstone apartment. Even in the dark, they glowed ghostlike in the moonlight, beckoning me to come closer more with all the subtle calling of a crooked finger waggling in my direction. Beckoning me to come.

Only, her fingers were motionless. I came anyway.

I had waited so long, and there they were. Even as I slumped half asleep against the park bench in front of her building, the messenger bag strapped across my shoulder like an empty embrace, I knew it was her.

***

IT ALL STARTED one evening in The Strand. From behind a tower of books, I watched as those fingers curled around the edges of a worn paperback, the top corners folded into soft, cottony folds from endless dog-earring. I watched as, without hesitation, she brought the book to the counter and purchased it anyway, slipping her delicate fingers into a clasp-topped coin purse up to the second knuckle to fish out the quarters and dimes she used to buy it.

I did the only thing I could do when confronted with such Pygmalion perfection. I followed her home.

Under the veil of a Manhattan twilight, it was easy enough. I just pulled out my cell phone and pretended to talk to someone on my empty list of friends as I stalked my prey along the rain-mottled streets of New York. It is simple to be invisible in the city. A pebble in a pond.

I remember watching her naked legs swish under the blue cotton skirt that fell just above her knee. Her shoes, these patent leather mary janes with a tiny blue flower pattern printed across the wedge heel, spattered in the thin puddles that veiled the pavement. Spring flowers bursting out of the cracked cement, the unstoppable force of nature.

She was my flower, my graceful willow tree stretching toward the sky. Toward me. She was my Daphne; I , her female Apollo, only she had chased me into chasing her. It was her fault. Her moon pale skin, the curve of her naked calves, those long-fingered hands. How could I resist?

And then she turned from the sidewalk and clattered up the smooth cement stairs, her hand trailing along the wrought iron railing until she mounted the platform outside the door. Fingers dipped into a pocket and pulled out a key. Key into lock. And then she was gone.

But it was enough. Now, I knew where she lived.

I followed her every night for six weeks after that—every night until tonight. This night that changed my world. Your world.

For six weeks, I followed her through the city, shadowed her at diners, watched her eating in the park during her lunch break from the office. I watched as she laughed with her boyfriend or rolled her eyes while she talked on the phone with her father. I followed her every night because I wanted her to notice me, to look at the round of my breasts beneath my blouse and see my eyes past the curtain of my brown hair. It wasn't just that, either. I wanted her to want me, too. I wanted her to want to press her cold hands on my body, to push her bony fingers inside me. I wanted her.

The way father wanted mother, I think, the night she died. The coroner had begged father to let another mortician handle mother's body. *The accident was too brutal,* he had said. *You should let someone else care for her now.* But father was nothing if he was not insistent with his cold stoicism. He stared blankly at the coroner, unmoving, until he had no choice but to leave the zippered leather bag in the preparation room of my father's mortuary, stretched across the stainless steel table with all the grace and ritual of a bag of laundry.

Father had told me to go up to my room and go to sleep. *This is no place for a child,* he had said; but, I only half-listened to him as, numbed by the shock of my mother's death, I padded through the door in my footie pajamas and closed it all but an inch so I could watch mother through the crack. I wanted to see her move her fingers, wriggle her toes, bat her eyes. I wanted to see that she wasn't really dead.

But instead, I watched as my father unzipped the bag full circle and slid mother's blue, shoeless foot from it. As her heel wobbled on the stainless steel, I rubbed my own toes as if to warm my mother's skin through my own.

After father had slid mother's naked body from the bag, he stared at her for a long time. She didn't move, not even a finger twitch, as he finally brought his hands down to rest on her head. He caressed her skin with his fingertips and I swear I saw a single, crystalline tear slide down his cheek, over his chin, and drop with a tiny splash on mother's forehead.

The coroner had closed mother's eyes, I guess, because father gently opened them and gazed into them. Then, he dipped his head to hers and pressed his lips to mother's. He fumbled with his belt buckle and his trousers dropped below his knees.

In silence, I watched as he completed the business of a husband and wife while my mother lay lifeless on the table. I could not look away. I was as transfixed by this tender act of love as much as I was disgusted at seeing, for the first time, my parents in this way. In that moment, though, I knew the truth of romance, and that was enough to keep me watching. Learning.

When he was through, he stood, pausing for a long time, still naked, still gazing at mother's body. At long last, he walked on bare feet across the ceramic-tiled floor I knew to be so cold. He stopped at the counter and opened a drawer. His hand reached inside and pulled out a pair of shining silver sheers such as those used by seamstresses and tailors. Turning back to mother, he snipped the sheers mindlessly in the air as if testing their strength to cut through vapor, and slid back across the floor.

In a flash, he swooped the sheers toward her head, snipping

quickly under the cold, fluorescent lights. Then, he placed the sheers by her head and brought his hand up toward his face, a lock of mother's hair clenched between his fingers. He breathed in her scent in one long inhalation before pressing the curl into his mouth and swallowing it down in one, dry gulp.

Everything in my life could be traced back to that night as the source of me. The night I discovered the meaning of love. The night I first understood what it meant to need someone so much that you had to eat her up, devour her piece by piece until you were insider her and she was inside you. That night was the single most important night of my existence.

Until tonight.

I'm not sure what it was exactly that brought her and I to this moment. Her endless flirting, perhaps? Those long nights of her always walking away from me so that I could see the sway of her hips, the cool skin of her legs, the bounce of her hair against the small of her back? Perhaps it was that silent, coy pleading in her eyes right before I plunged into her with the knife? Or the wet smack of her lips freckled with blood as she whispered for me to stop toying with her.

She wanted it so badly. I could see it in her eyes. She wanted me to bring her to completion, so I did. I tore off my blouse, exposing my small, pert breasts that pointed slightly upward at the nipples. I wrestled off my denim skirt and climbed on top of her, slipping my fingers between the soft folds of her vulva, wet now with the blood that spilled over her stomach and down the grooves of her inner thighs.

As I showed her my undying love, I watched the light slip from her eyes. I pressed my mouth to her lips and kissed her, and as I stretched out her two forefingers and pressed them inside of me, I began to think about my mother and her mother and so on backward through history until my mind warbled around the plague and the deaths of millions in ancient days, the days of my ancestors—of all our ancestors.

And as I rocked back and forth against her lifeless wrist, I began to realize the infinity of my life and love as I knew that I was comprised of a genetic structure predisposed to survivalism. My blood makes the antibodies to destroy cholera, the Black Death. My beloved. Me. Anti-body. Body against itself.

These thoughts filled me as I reached orgasm, and with them, the eternal tragedy of romance—always to pine, never to be requited. One lives, one dies. Death separates us into these nauseating pockets of isolation and love becomes an ache inside our hearts. The way I love her.

And now, as I stare at her pale, bloodless face, her eyes gazing up at the pressed tin ceiling of her apartment, I know that I always will.

She will always be with me.

I reach into my bag and pull out a pair of shiny silver sheers, snipping the air as I bring them toward me. They are sharp enough to cut vapor as I place her two fingers just below the second knuckle between the blades and snap them closed. The bones of her fingers fight against the blades, but a few tries and they finally give way to my desires, falling with a spurt of blood into my open palm.

Without hesitation, I drop the sheers and flip open my bag to reveal the array of surgical tools sewn into loops inside the front flap. I select a scalpel, sliding it out of the elastic loops and pressing it into the groove of my thumb like a pencil. Sucking in a breath, I drag the sharp end across my breast, just above my heart. A slash of red spreads beneath my breast in a curve that reminds me of the smile of a clown before it drips down my belly in tiny rivers of blood.

The pain is intense, but this is my homage to her. This is my poem. My opus. My pure golden love that howls her name. It is the pain that is my gift to her.

I think of this as I use my fingertips to pry open the flesh of my breast before I stuff her fingers under my skin and pinch it closed as if I am trussing a chicken for roasting. I am gasping with pain and tears stream down my face as I reach blindly toward my bag with my hands, my fingers searching for the hooked sewing needle already prepared with thread.

Piercing the folds of my skin, I begin to sew her inside of me with each criss-crossed, black stitch. After the first two, shock seems to overcome the pain and I'm no longer aware of the sharp sting of the needle as it penetrates my skin.

My eyes are clear.

It is as I am tying off the last stitch, after biting the straggling end between my teeth, that I notice the plastic tub of pill bottles beneath the coffee table.

Strange, I think, as I pull the tub toward me, my left hand still clutching the red mess of my breast. My right hand swishes through the tub, smearing blood on the orange bottles, and I read the labels one by one.

There must be thirty bottles here, I think, as I tally off the ones I know and try to imagine the uses for the ones I don't. Pain killers, anti-psychotics, anti-anxieties. Beneath the bottles, I find a handful of plastic-sheathed syringes and glass vials of liquid. One is bright green as if she'd siphoned the fluid from inside a neon highlighter pen. Another is a familiar yellow and I recognize it immediately.

Formaldehyde?

But before the question can completely form in my mind, I am choking back a stomach full of black bile and bloody vomit. It spills effortlessly from between my clenched teeth, filling the plastic tub with the contents of my guts.

My eyes roll backward into my head and white film seems to veil my eyes. I can barely breathe as I gasp for air, sucking in mouthfuls of my own vomit instead. As the last beats of my heart pound against my chest, I caress the two, bony lumps beneath my breast where her fingers are inside me, where her blood mingles with my own. Where she and I are connected forever in spite of this life, or this death that our love has wrought.

And I feel relief, knowing she is there with me as I take my final, drowning breath of bile. Through white, filmy vision, I look toward her fallen form and watch her. I am looking at what is left of her fingers. I want to see her move her fingers, her toes wriggle, her eyes bat the air. I want to see that she isn't really dead.

And her fingers twitch. *They're moving.* She must not really be dead, but how? How can . . . ?

And then it hits me. Even as my lungs fill with liquid, even as my throat constricts and my nearly every corner of my mind focuses on the burning feeling in my throat and lungs, I am able to form this final thought as I watch her hand twitch and then press into the floor as her body jerks marionette-like to its feet, her cold and empty eyes staring down at me vacantly.

Of course, she is not dead—just released from her prison of medication. And from her fingers under my skin, I too am freed from the bondage of this life. And when I awaken from this sleep of death, what dreams may come as we—she and I—show the whole world the power of our *undying* love.

Tonight, I will rise a new woman, if a corpse. And together, my undead love and I will discover what it means to need someone so much that you must eat her up, devour her piece by piece until you are inside her and she is inside you. And when my love and I are done, the whole world will feel the sting of our love as we slip inside of you. Under your skin.

GENESIS ABMORTAL

BENJAMIN MOORE

SILVER MOONLIGHT DRIFTS tumbled through loose curtains. Jasmine blooms covered the breeze with a delicate fragrance. A sensual, mid-spring evening called to amorous couples everywhere. Kitchen floor squeaked, table legs creaked. Janelle and Justin became one.

The pale light withered on Janelle's pallid chest. Her porcelain skin and dark twinkly eyes didn't stand out the way they used to. Sunken, black, vacuous pits swallowed the glimmer. When she looked at her husband that connection, that bond between souls, vanished. Like she looked upon the chair or counter top, nothing deeper.

"So, is this doing anything for you?" Justin asked.

"Not really. Nope. It feels pointless. Like we're just going through the motions."

"I know. I thought the same thing."

"Should we continue?"

"Hold on . . . . Yep . . . . That's it. I'm done."

"How do you know?"

"It felt like I peed. I can keep going if you want."

"No, that's okay. Despite your sexy talk, it's just not the same. Hell, even our worst sex was better than this."

"I know."

"Did you ever imagine you'd have a last time?"

"Never. I figured I'd take enough ED meds to stop my heart long before I ever lost my boner. This rigor mortis thing seemed cool at first, but there's no pleasure. Just cruel irony."

"Yeah, I had some high hopes for you as well. Get off me."

And so Janelle and Justin became two.

Life after death was existence. No joy, no sorrow, no purpose to get up in the morning. No reason to go to bed at night.

Hunger motivated them. Endless want that resembled their usual nutritional drive, though no matter how much they ate they never got full. Theirs was a hunger not of the stomach, but of the soul—or lack of one.

Janelle and Justin stayed together, shared in each other's existence, but as with their last escapade, both participated out of inertia instead of love. Deep feelings between them shallowed. Each regarded their spouse with little more interest than animals passing in the night.

That sense of kinship evanesced, but they still remembered. They recalled how fulfilled and happy they once lived ensconced in reciprocated desire. Those sweet, long-lost memories kept them together. That feeling, the joy they once felt was what they hungered for, though neither could articulate those needs.

Justin stared at his betrothed across the dinner table. She once stirred such emotion in him he'd say the stupidest things to see her smile. Wide with a pair of dimples at the corners and a bright crescent of teeth. Janelle had an infectious smile, one that spread to every person in her realm.

He remembered it, but couldn't recall the last time she smiled. Justin couldn't even think of the last time they laughed together. Nothing good, or bad, had occurred since that night a few weeks earlier when everything around their town had died—sort of.

Some piece of everything died. Something important to life, yet not mechanical. Muscles flexed, though they moved like soggy sand. Hearts beat arithmetically. Lungs functioned, but breath didn't seem necessary.

Janelle ate her portion of Justin's bounty. She consumed to satiate that heinous hunger. Justin, too, scooped a morsel of a woman's brain into his mouth without regard. He remembered the woman's screams, the sheer terror in her eyes as he ripped out her throat. Blood sprayed across his face, blurred his vision. A few beats later, by the time he rubbed enough away to see, her body had lost pressure. The rest dribbled out until she died. That crack of stone against skull, like a hammer to a coconut, rattled in his head, but none of this bothered Justin. It would've a few weeks earlier, but not now. Now he couldn't identify with frightened victims, he only needed their brains.

Janelle examined Justin as well. His bright blue eyes clouded over, opaque and milky, like cataracts covered his thirty-two-year-old irises. Crusty blood cracked and flaked away from his jaw as he chewed. Dreaded mats of bloody hair lay pasted and messy. He looked homeless, lifeless.

"So did it fight?" Janelle didn't know why she asked. She didn't care, the information wouldn't intrigue or entertain her. She recalled asking questions about Justin's day when they used to eat together.

"Yep. She must have known karate or something. Punched me in the face a dozen times."

"Hmmm."

"She had a kid with her, too. Another zombie got it, though."

"Is that what we are?"

"Zombies? I don't know. I'm eating some lady's raw brain. I'm not sure what else to call myself," Justin said.

Janelle finished her portion. "Why do we even eat this stuff? I wouldn't have touched a brain before, not even cooked, but now I don't want anything else."

"Maybe because that was the last thing their souls touched."

"I don't know what a soul tastes like."

"I bet our zombie taste buds do."

"Quiet Justin. Don't call me a zombie."

"Why, does it offend you?"

"No, but it would've a few weeks ago."

A few weeks ago . . .

The turning point for Justin, Janelle and a hundred neighbors in their forest town of Wynona came when kooky cultists down the road blew themselves to smithereens. All time references from then on called back to that moment as the qualifying event every activity, experience or incident occurred before or after.

"Have you noticed how bad the yard has gotten?"

"Yeah. It looks like a foreclosure," Justin mumbled through a mouthful of frontal lobe.

"Can you at least turn the sprinklers on tomorrow?"

"Why?"

"Because it would've disgusted me a few weeks ago."

"So do it because we used to do it. Got it."

The sprinklers came on, the yard was cleaned, the house maintained. Janelle and Justin went about their lives as if nothing had changed. But it had. A fine yard once brought pride. A clean home once welcomed guests. Both motivations vanished.

Janelle would phone her mother every day, though a few weeks earlier the conversation changed. Instead of their usual gossip about babies, siblings or girlie biology, Janelle's mother's tone ground down to scorn as she berated the pervert that kept calling only to groan at her for an hour. Janelle tried to reassure her mother she was no pervert, but her mother wouldn't listen. She wondered if dementia might have touched her mother's mind. The last phone call Janelle made received an automated reply—her mother had blocked her number. It confused Janelle, but it didn't sadden her. That emotion disappeared with happiness.

All jokes aside, foreclosure entered their future. Justin lost his job after he'd shown up late for work and ate his boss's brain. He'd always walked on thin ice, but the HR couldn't overlook that transgression. Justin called several times to plead his case, beg for his job, yet he never got passed reception.

"Stop calling or I'll notify police!" the receptionist screamed.

That was the last thing Justin heard from a company he'd given ten years of his life. It didn't disappoint him like it should've, though.

He went on a few interviews afterward, but those always ended in shouts and brainings. Justin had to face it. At some point he'd become unemployable.

"I think I'll hike up to that cult compound. Poke around a little," Justin said.

"You won't find anything interesting."

"Maybe. I saw several sets of headlights over there the other day. Besides, most everyone has fled Wynona. Only the drunks are left and you know how they upset my stomach. I'll head off toward Oaksburg tomorrow night, but first I'd like to check someplace closer."

"Yes, dear."

***

A FAINT SCENT carried over the damp breeze. The aroma Justin recognized. Stray rays filtered through the pine canopy, glowing golden beams solidified on a gathered bank of fog. Woodsy odors settled in cool morning air, but this peculiar scent rose into the atmosphere with heat. Body heat.

People explored at the exploded cult compound. Justin knew it. He could smell their souls.

A bestial hunger took over. His senses sharpened. Leaf litter cracked beneath his feet, but Justin stayed out of sight.

Behind a tree.

Quick glance.

Creep a little closer.

The heavy fog tamped small sounds. Justin weaved around the tree line, got a count and saw how they concentrated. That building's remains held more interest to them than the forest.

Yellow caution tape outlined their investigation scene as if that fluttery plastic could stop a hungry predator. One sheriff with a shotgun, two FBI agents picking through debris and a photographer. That sheriff's weapon presented a problem. The agents certainly carried side arms, but nothing scared a zombie more than a shotgun.

Justin sneaked behind the sheriff still within the forest. He picked up a handful of weighty rocks, threw one hard against a tree, skipped another under some dried pine needles. The noises sounded intentional. Another rock scattered a clump of pinecones.

The agents took notice. The photographer's attention followed. The sheriff stepped to inspect.

With the shotgun hung lazily at his side, the sheriff cast a suspicious gaze into the foggy woods. His keen insight on local flora and fauna along with the weapon settled enough of the agents' concerns that they went back to their ruins.

Justin had the sheriff chasing noises. But the sheriff wasn't a dope. He didn't run after the first thing he heard.

A couple more rocks into the leaves, another pitched hard at a tree trunk. The muted thud echoed. His suspicions piqued, the sheriff circled around the noisy source. Shotgun stock nested against his shoulder, eyes darted over portly cheeks. He softened his steps, padded through the litter, listening for more noise.

Justin threw a rock straight up into the canopy. A woody thump rustled pine needles, bird wings flapped. The sheriff drew his gun skyward, caught sight of the rock and watched it drop to Justin's feet.

Before his shotgun caught up to his fright, Justin jumped from behind the tree, stone held high, and smashed the sheriff's head.

That sheriff's melon cracked wide open. White fog simmered off the warm gray. Justin dug in and scooped up a handful of steamy brains. The sticky mush placated his carnal hunger, but it didn't satisfy his endless want. He smelled it, tasted its residue, but Justin couldn't eat the sheriff's soul. No matter how much he ate or how fresh the brain, Justin couldn't fill that hole inside—he couldn't replace his soul.

Those agents wouldn't wait long. Justin gobbled up another handful. He snatched the shotgun and took the sheriff's shoes. A thicket across the way offered another opportunity for a ravenous zombie to snare his prey.

Their souls smelled good. Especially hers. The female agent stooped over. Justin had a perfect view of her big ol' butt; her tawny skin, the way her vest rounded over her pleasant breasts. Justin liked a little meat on the bones. Before two weeks ago, this woman's form would've aroused him. She would've caught too much of his attention.

Wait.

Yes.

Justin felt tightness against his pants. That woman, the FBI agent did it. He felt . . . rigor mortis, nothing else.

Justin tossed one shoe into a bush. Obvious to a trained investigator, yet hidden enough to illicit abstract caution. He threw the other shoe in a spot to draw their attention toward the sheriff's body and tiptoed behind another tree.

It took those stuck-up FBI agents over ten minutes to figure out their sheriff escort hadn't returned. They called for him, searched the perimeter, found the lone shoe.

Pistols came out. The agents scanned for threats. One rounded the bushes with the second swinging wide for back-up. The second spotted the other shoe. With the rear of the bush clear, they scanned their path ahead. That's when the sheriff's body came into view. The first agent stood beside the second. They discussed the wider scene, estimated ambush points and probable retreats.

Justin stood close enough to hear them whisper. A tremble of fear hitched in their throats.

Justin threw another rock into the forest. A sharp rap of stone to wood snapped the agents' heads left. Justin sprung from the right. He blasted one agent point blank in the chest, cycled the shotgun, trained it on the other. Before the female agent returned fire, Justin shot her right between those pleasant breasts.

At such close range the shotgun's sheer force smashed their body armor and collapsed their hearts.

The photographer shouted. Justin broke for the sound. He ran into the clearing straight for the last person. The photographer fled toward the tree line.

Justin fired a round far outside a shotgun's range. At least one of those third-of-an-inch, buckshot pellets struck the photographer in the back. He stumbled over, tripped on a tree root.

Justin pumped his shotgun. The man climbed to his feet and ran for it, but that time on the ground gave up most of his lead.

Justin fired again. This time many more pellets struck with much greater force.

The photographer didn't go down. He stayed on his feet and booked it for the trees, though some of those pellets penetrated a calf. The man pulled up lame. Justin caught him and put a full load of buckshot in the photographer's back.

Lead shattered vertebrae.

That did it. That finished the photographer.

With the butt of his shotgun, Justin ever so gingerly cracked open the photographer's skull. He picked away a few boney shards and shook out the brain intact.

Janelle had complained that Justin only brought home mush. This whole piece would be a nice surprise.

Justin wrapped his bounty in a jacket, strolled over to the FBI agents and plucked their brains with just as much care. For a midmorning snack he excavated what remained in the sheriff's head as well.

As Justin strolled home, he spotted a book amidst the cult compound rubble. Singed, a little torn, but otherwise in good shape.

Necropedia Britanica blazed in crimson Old English against a carbon-black cover.

That would've caught his curiosity before, so Justin plucked it from the debris and carried it home along with the brains to his wife.

***

"OOOOH, YOU'RE GOING to get some tonight." Even though neither received pleasure, Janelle always used to reward Justin properly whenever he exceeded her expectations.

"Why wait?" Justin asked with typical bravado.

To indulge in a whole brain indeed pleased Janelle—sort of. She and Justin got down and dirty. They gorged during sex, ate beyond healthy capacity, tried by any physical measures to fill that emptiness within, though no contorted positions or twisted fetishes seemed to work.

Justin backed away, Janelle rolled off the kitchen table. They took their usual seat across from each other to finish the meal.

"Hey, I picked up a present for your fat gothic sister," Justin said through a mushy mouthful.

"Don't be mean. She's not fat. She's just going through a thing right now."

"She's pretty fat for whatever thing she's going through. Anyway, I found this." Justin slid the book across the table.

"*Necropedia Britanica?*"

"Yeah, I thought there might be something in there so she could become a real zombie, like us."

"She wants to be a vampire, not a zombie. Geez, get it right."

"Of course. What fat chick wouldn't want to be the sexier undead?" Justin said sarcastically.

Janelle thumbed through the pages. Flecks of charred paper stuck to her blood-tackied fingers. The *Necropedia Britanica* fell open to the most used section of the thousand page tome. "And lo," Janelle read aloud, "His gift shall be passed from parents, two, to child. The gifted shall bequeath His gift in an unbroken chain. For it is unto His children of form that this gift of soul first be presented and it is this union of body and soul that forms in His image the creature mortal. Be warned ye mortal who wishes not receive His gift, for to break the chain is to damn all joy, to damn all relief from suffering, to damn mortality . . . "

"So those stupid cultists blew themselves up trying to become immortal?" Justin asked.

"The recipe that follows is called, 'Abmortality.' It doesn't sound like they wanted to live forever, just spite God by rejecting their souls. Check this out, 'Ash from thine caldron breathed shall whither His gift and deplete the eternal moiety of mortal form.' Remember the ash cloud that settled after their compound exploded?"

"Yeah. So we're abmortal, huh? Not as much fun as it sounds."

Janelle and Justin went back to their meal. They ate in contemplative silence with only an impression of sorrow to draw on. Neither expressed a genuine sensation of loss. Both knew they should be upset, but they weren't. That hole where their souls once resided became a pit of inexpressible anxiety, where emotions went to mature, yet fell into a moral morass. Good, bad, happy, sad lost all true meaning. They became words in sound only.

***

AS HE HAD in mortality, Justin went out to bring home the daily bread. A second trip to the obliterated cult compound yielded more rewards. The FBI sent another team to investigate their agents' disappearances.

Eventually the FBI cut their losses and when they stopped investigating, Justin headed south to Oaksburg. The semi-rural population was easy to hunt. Just big enough that any pockets of concern couldn't coordinate to evacuate or attack, yet small enough to provide without excessive travel. Those poor townsfolk, with all their shotguns, became skittish, timid, perfect victims for hungry zombies.

Sometimes a pickup truck with a bed full of gun totin' yahoos patrolled Oaksburg streets, but they added a false sense of safety to the community. People put down their guard when those pickups drove by. Justin hid in the shadows until they moved along. He'd creep through the front door, invade people's homes and take their tasty brains. He got good, real good. Justin could get into any home and take what he wanted before shotguns came into play.

After one haul, with his fare spread across the table, ready for his reward, Janelle announced, "I'm pregnant."

"What! How do you know?"

"I just do."

"Did you miss your period? Have you been vomiting your brains out? Any strange cravings? I can pick up some pickles or peanut butter when I go back into town tomorrow night."

"I don't remember when I last menstruated, I haven't been vomiting, no cravings. I just know it."

"So are you happy?"

"I don't actually care."

The notion of parenthood gripped them both. In the days before, they wanted children, made plans and waited for the right situation. They were still a year away, but their time was almost at hand. Since the cult compound explosion, their desires for the family way died with their souls. Both Janelle and Justin remembered those desires. They knew they should feel joy, yet nothing came to either.

"So, I guess you're eating for two now?"

"I guess."

"I can't wait until your boobs get bigger." Justin wanted to say that for so long and at one point in his life he truly meant it. Now he didn't care. He hadn't touched his wife's breasts in weeks and felt no real urges to do so in the future, no matter how big they got.

Justin went out foraging all the same. Janelle's belly grew as it should. Both thought they wanted this to be the greatest experience people said it was, but neither took any joy. That pit, left behind as poison ash murdered their souls, swallowed any hints of emotion. They couldn't even feel sad for not feeling happy. Ambivalence proved a harsher curse than any sorrow or shame ever leveled against a mortal human being.

***

OAKSBURG'S POPULATION THINNED. People moved out and those that stayed brought better defenses against intruders. Pickup truck patrols coordinated with law enforcement to cover larger areas of the town. Their synchronized efforts stymied Justin's attempts to put food on his table.

Justin thought about Big Acorn Valley, but that town lay another thirty miles south. He'd have to consider vehicular transportation for forays down there. That meant staying on roads, that meant being seen, that meant trouble.

Janelle's breasts grew. So did the rest of her, but Justin never noticed. She looked like the desiccated wisp of a zombie that waited for him every day since their souls perished. Janelle, too, ignored the physical changes. She felt no compulsions to mind her nutrition or build an adequate nest. As if nothing had changed, she went on with her mundane existence.

"Hey, what is this?"

"It's all I could find," Justin explained. "They sicced a dog on me. I barely had time to strip it before those yahoos started shooting at me."

"What do you think I am? I'm not going to eat any part of a dog! Smell it. Have you smelled it?! It stinks!"

"I know, I know. I had to bring *some*thing home."

"I refuse to feed my baby dog brains. Now you go down to Big Acorn Valley and pick up something decent."

"Yes, dear."

***

THE CLOSEST VEHICLES Justin could nab that wouldn't raise immediate attention sat at the exploded cult compound. He'd managed to scare off enough people that the FBI left their cars behind when they gave up the site.

Wild animals had cleaned most of what remained. Raggedy jackets and torn pants lay all around. A quick shake here or there jingled several sets of keys.

Of the half dozen vehicles available, a white sedan seemed the most inconspicuous. Justin drove the two mile long dirt road, through Wynona, past Oaksburg and down to Big Acorn Valley.

The site of all those people going about their business without an eye squinted sideways for caution led Justin to a passive hope he didn't expect. He'd put real food on the table for Janelle tonight. Justin drove down Main Street, doubled back and drifted into a residential neighborhood. Plenty of high hedges and old oak trees offered the silent stalker enough cover to conduct his gruesome chores.

Two houses, set next to each other, looked like perfect targets. Easy access between both, a street behind them, an on-ramp to the highway nearby with lots of foliage around to spoil errant screams. Justin typically didn't hit two houses at a time for safety reasons, but Big Acorn Valley lay so far away he might as well make the trip worthwhile.

Day crumbled to night. House lights flickered out as people rambled off to bed. Justin parked behind the houses. He slid among shadows, disappeared into the darkness and followed his instincts toward a sleepy home. No one locked the backdoor. No one ever had to.

Their mistake.

The home smelled rich and warm, like a bakery of souls. Three, four, six distinct scents. Two stories, children's effects around. Justin chose well. He crept into the master bedroom. A father and mother slept side by side. A poignant thought entered Justin's murderous mind. Those two resembled a fantasy of him and Janelle. Happy heads of a loving home. The sentiment almost put a smile on his face as he bashed the man's skull open.

The lady screamed. Justin, with one hand, ripped out her throat. She collapsed and gurgled her last breaths.

Justin went through the rest of the house collecting the low fruit. He paused and admired all the toys in each child's room. Girls' toys, boys' toys, decorations, books. All those things his own child should have. That would come later, though. He had work to do.

The second house proved more bountiful than the first. He cleared out both homes in less than half an hour. Justin had a whole sack full of brains, most intact.

That should get him a piece. His standard incentive for exceptional achievements.

Into the sedan, onto the highway and headed north without any suspicions raised. Big Acorn Valley might work out after all.

Justin made the long trip home. Janelle's nose perked up the second he stepped through the door. "Good, you brought back . . . . You've been busy." She pulled back a hideous, decayed smile that signaled sex to come.

"It's a long trip. I don't think I can handle the commute every day."

"That's okay. We can adjust. Hey, it's started."

"What?"

"Labor."

"Does it hurt?"

"No," Janelle replied, as she tore into a sloppy, cold brain.

"What do you want to name it?"

"If it's a girl, I'll name it lunch. If it's a boy, I'll name it dinner."

"You'd eat your own baby? That's wicked."

"You have a better plan?"

"Nope. At least we won't have to save for college."

Janelle's labor lasted all of three hours. A tiny baby boy sprung into the world from the loins of death. Justin held up his son, counted all his fingers and toes, examined the tiny child as it transitioned to an aerobic, light filled environment. Its creaky short screeches did nothing to ignite sympathy or warmth in his parents. Quite the opposite. They both had designs on its delicate brain.

"Let me hold it," Janelle said. Justin handed the boy to his hungry mom. She brought him to her face, sniffed at his head and licked the pulsating soft spot. The infant cried out for his mother, but that newborn noise didn't distract Janelle.

"You notice something?" Justin asked. "It doesn't look rotten. It looks . . . healthy. Why doesn't it look desiccated?"

"I don't know," Janelle answered. "It doesn't smell right either."

"It's just that new-baby smell."

"No, I mean I don't smell a soul."

Justin leaned in and sniffed at the baby boy as well. "It's not a zombie like us, but it has no soul either."

"It's a true abmortal," Janelle said.

"I don't care what it is. I'm going to leave it out for the coyotes."

"Hurry back, tiger, and we'll do it." Janelle struck a sexy pose, laid out across the kitchen table, head held in a hand, propped up on an elbow, one leg open and inviting.

Justin eyed his prize. The mottled gray placenta fell out. "I'll be back in a minute."

With his baby under an arm, Justin opened the front door to take care of business when one of the yahoos stepped up and blew his head clean off. The baby fell with his father's twice-dead corpse. The yahoos stormed the house and blasted Janelle. She flew off the table beneath the lead rain. One more round splattered her head against the wooden floor.

A supervising FBI agent followed behind his conscripted yahoos. Never had a crime scene horrified him more. Those *zombies* had almost eaten a newborn baby. The agent's mortal sympathy raged as he swaddled the infant in his windbreaker, cuddled it to his armored chest with spiteful diligence.

Behind the overwhelming scent of his own soul, the agent couldn't detect the abmortal seed's deficiency. Its tiny squeak and cold, jerky limbs kindled a nurturing response. The agent promised to protect the child, to cherish and love this helpless victim for the rest of his life—though he should've spent another shotgun shell to protect mortality instead.

PHASE

JAY WILBURN

"BATTERIES, BATTERIES, I need batteries," he hissed.

He had a strict rule against talking out loud that he broke regularly. This wasn't his house and he had not searched it very well. There could be one in a closet or in a room he had overlooked. He was getting sloppy in so many ways and not getting killed was making him careless.

He needed double A batteries. He needed 8 of them. Why 8? If it was going to take 8, why not use a bigger, damn battery? There were C's and D's.

He found some triple A's in a kid's toy in the living room. God, he hoped there wasn't a kid still in here. Kids were creepy before, but he absolutely hated them now.

He found some nine volts in the smoke detectors. They were starting to go dead. He could tell because they were beeping every few seconds. It was more obvious when the lack of power took away every other sound in the house.

Everything in the world was going dead or was already there.

He even found two of those little disc, spare watch batteries still in the packages. Who has the foresight to buy two spare watch batteries, but has no double A's?

Keith had never in his life seen a B battery, but he expected to find one in this house the way things were going.

Finally, he hurled the digital camera against the wall. He regretted it the moment it left his hand. It left a gash in the dry wall at the end of the island where the kitchen opened into the hallway. It broke into far more pieces than he expected, but it wasn't nearly as satisfying as he would have hoped.

Nothing was nearly as satisfying as he hoped anymore.

Every picture he had taken was lost to him. What a waste! It took him weeks to figure out how to use the camera in the first place. He was closing in on 50 years old now and he had not embraced technology well. He would have still been using a film camera, if he could find one. He would also need to find a working pharmacy because he couldn't develop pictures either.

He knew how to check e-mail, but that was a wasted skill now. He had never used a computer that someone else hadn't hooked up for him first. Not that that mattered anymore either he supposed.

The worst part about technology was it had eliminated magazines. It had eliminated the ones he was looking for anyway. He could find a *Maxim* every once and a while, but that did him no good at all. He had gone into a convenience store once or twice looking for something better, but there was nothing.

When he was a kid, he used to sneak over to his friend's house because his dad had the Playboy Channel. It came on after 8:00 P.M. and showed cable edited stuff in the early eighties. A bunch of guys would sit around and watch while trying to pretend no one else was in the room.

Once the Internet came around, finding what he needed got a lot easier as an adult. It made Keith wish he had ditched his old VHS tapes a long time ago and got someone to show him how to use the Internet sooner.

His mom had walked in on him once when he was a kid trying to watch scrambled stuff on the old fashioned cable boxes late at night. His parents had come up with some kind of lock after that and then it was a long dry spell for him.

They never talked about it, but he did hear his mom whisper to his dad once that it was just a phase.

The Internet provided a whole new phase in his own living room as a grown man. He found out he needed a lot more than the stuff they used to show after 8:00 in the 1980's. And there was a lot more to be found too.

After the zombies came along, the power was out, food was scarce, and his favorite hobby was shut off. Every bit of it was in the form of technology and as usual, technology had bitten him right where it hurt the most.

Memory was enough to sustain Keith for a while.

This was probably just a phase. It was just another dry spell. The smart guys that knew about technology would figure out how to get rid of the zombies and get the Internet back on soon enough.

He could take care of himself. He played solitaire. He found cans to eat from cold. He could hide and sleep in houses he couldn't afford in real life. He could run short distances to get away from the walking dead, if he had to do it. He could use memory to pass the time, if he got bored, but that did not last.

Memory faded fast and it only got worse the longer the dry spell lasted.

Once he got really bored, he started to notice the zombies. A lot of them were dudes. They were mangled up and grotesque. A lot of them were dragging what was left of themselves through the streets looking for something to eat. They were looking for Keith to eat. They didn't have stomachs sometimes, but they were nothing but hungry. Food was as useless to them as B batteries or a digital camera with no power, but they would chew off every piece of him.

Some of them were chicks.

A few of them still had clothes and arms, but they had lost all modesty. Sometimes their clothes would slide just a little to tease him. Sometimes they were baring all just like those joints that advertised along the Interstate on the way to Florida.

He started to find that even when their skin was the wrong color, or they had gashes across their bodies, or they were painted in dark stains, or they were missing big pieces, as long as they had a few of the right pieces left, they could still do the trick.

Keith was in a dry spell. It was just a phase and it was only to tide him over for a while.

He had a couple beauties go right by the window of a Dairy Queen he had been hiding in for a few hours to let a thick mob of the dead go on by him. Aside from the huge chunks bitten out of them, they could have been living, breathing porn stars. They actually were breathing. They were moaning too which had helped. One of them had one of those lower back tattoos he had never seen in real life before then. He hadn't felt that good since the first day he discovered the fetish sites.

Then, it was just one long parade of dudes. It was like they had opened the hotdog stand outside the Dairy Queen. He was trapped there for hours. It was almost dark before it cleared up enough for him to escape. The smell of rotten meat inside the abandoned restaurant had not helped.

That was the start of a long, dry spell.

Keith had seen nothing, but guy zombies for two weeks. He started traveling around trying to find more groups, but the ladies were absent. The memory of his porn stars was fading fast and he didn't have a lot of options.

He had gotten the idea for the camera then. He started taking pictures from the windows and using them later when he needed. After a while, he started going out and getting closer.

Eventually, he ran right up to the beauties and started getting the super close-ups like he used to find on the web. The best part of zombie babes was that they would follow him anywhere. He could walk backwards, taking his time, and checking the camera until he had gotten the perfect pose.

One time, he had stumbled into a group of the monsters as he was trying to walk backwards from a chubby corpse in a sagging bikini and he nearly got torn apart. He was shaking when he got to safety and started checking himself for bites or scratches. The excitement and terror had done the trick. Once he was sure he hadn't been infected, he just left his clothes off and took care of business. He barely needed the pictures from the tiny camera screen at all.

That was the start of his chasing phase.

After a while, he got bored with that too. He was smart enough and scared enough not to try to let them grab him more. He had to come up with something new.

The new game became stripping down the zombies and getting his pictures. He did not like the smell. He had to use nose plugs or the smell ruined it for him. Sometimes he found nasty surprises when he pulled off their clothes. Bad things happened when a person died and worse things happened when decaying bodies decided to walk around. With a little persistence though, he would get a good shot that would satisfy him for a day or two.

The next phase was goosing. That is what it was called when he was in school back when they were doing it to living girls. They got in surprisingly little trouble for it when he was a boy. Kids probably went to jail for it now. Well, now most kids were creepy, groaning dead things. He almost got bitten for it, but that was part of the thrill.

Some of their parts were soft. Some were like rocks. Every once and a while he got to feel implants. He never got to do that before the zombies rose. He wondered if they felt different on living women. Sometimes the flesh nearly sloughed right off of them under his fingers like the skin off a boiled pig. He had to use the nose plugs. It still made his eyes water and his stomach turn, but after a while, that was part of the thrill too.

He had used latex gloves at first, but that phase soon passed too.

Sometimes he would try to hold on longer before running off or taking the picture of him holding their parts like real women never let him. If he found one that was particularly uncoordinated or particularly photogenic, he would manipulate it into a pose that he could get a good rub through his clothes. It was always with his clothes on and then he would ditch whatever he was wearing. There was plenty of stuff his size lying around in closets. No need to keep ruined duds that were spoiled on one side or the other. There were no working washing machines anymore after all.

He had been fighting the next phase for some time now. There was no one around to talk sense into him and there was nothing else that interested him anymore.

"You know where this is going and you know it's going to end badly," Keith said out loud.

If he was going to smash cameras against walls, the no-talking-out-loud rule seemed a little bit of a waste. With everything else he was doing, trying to talk himself down seemed a little stupid too.

God, he missed the Internet. He missed refrigeration. He missed his jerky neighbors. He missed ice cream. He missed air conditioning sometimes and central heat other times. He missed hot, running water and flush toilets. He missed the smell of frying bacon and the smell of fresh air. He missed popcorn. He missed music. He missed crappy, rap music. He missed commercials. He missed drive-thrus. He missed Chinese food at the mall. He missed calendars with new pages. He even missed work and alarm clocks. He missed sitting in a dark basement pretending his friends weren't there listening for a car to pull up in the driveway while the Playboy Channel was on the old, cable box with the switches.

He missed his mother who cared enough to try to protect him from the dark things in the world and from the wrath of his father.

Life was just a phase and life had entered a definite, dry spell. Missing things was just a phase too.

There was another beep from the dying smoke detector. He would never miss that.

Keith shook himself out of his sadness and walked across the dark, stuffy kitchen. He dug through the pieces of technology that were shattered on the floor. He lifted out what he believed to be the memory card from the camera and he stuffed it in the pocket of the jeans that belonged to someone dead.

He looked out the front window from around the corner of the hallway. A few shapes drifted along outside through the lacy curtains. He saw a few shadows, but nothing that revealed what was waiting for him outside. There was a low moan, but that didn't tell him much either.

He looked back at the counter on the other side of the island in the room behind him. He finally found what he was looking for now that he had given up on the double A batteries. He picked it up and started for the front door.

Normally, he had the good sense to use side doors to slip out without being noticed, but a new phase called for new boldness and new rules.

He let his hand rest on the knob for a moment as he considered his choices.

He said out loud, "Keith, my boy, you are going to have some real fun now."

He held the butcher knife up and let the light gleam off of it from the dirty front window as best he could. It looked sharp, but there was only one way to find out. He was careful not to look at his own reflection in the blade. Seeing his own face ruined his mood worse than the smell from the zombies. He let the knife hang at his side again, but he held the handle hard enough to make his fingers ache.

Keith turned the knob and stepped out into the light.

I, ZOMBIE

JAKE CESARONE

I GRADUALLY STRUGGLED to my feet, brushing the clods of dirt from my trousers. I hurt everywhere, I was confused, and I was hungry.

Where was I? *Who* was I? I looked around. I was in a field of some sort, but I couldn't remember how I got here. There were trees, and shrubs, and many holes in the ground. There were also many other people, looking as confused as I was. They were moving—no, lurching—toward the west, toward the setting sun. I followed.

Moving with the crowd, I found that my legs were not working correctly. My knees would barely bend. So I walked, lurched, stiff-legged, along with the crowd, picking up speed and trying to keep up. My arms swung limply at my sides. I couldn't remember my name, where I was from, how I got here. But it didn't matter; all I knew was that I was still hungry, so very hungry!

I caught up with one tall thin fellow. Lumbering up to him, I tried to ask him where we were and where we were going. But no words came from my mouth, only grunts. I could form the thoughts in my mind, but my mouth would not utter them. He turned to look at me. Half of his jaw was missing, and his eyes were hollow in deep, dark sockets. He frightened me. I turned away, and continued lurching along with the crowd.

There was a group of people huddled on the ground, crouched around a moist black shape. I smelled food. I was so hungry. I went to them. On the ground in the center of the group was a heap of flesh; I could not tell what sort of animal it was from. Bones and flesh and entrails were everywhere, oozing gore. The group was reaching in, ripping out shreds of flesh with their hands, devouring them. I shouldered my way into the circle; I was so *hungry!* I reached into the bloody, fleshy mass and ripped out a handful of the greasy, slimy meat. I raised it to my mouth and fed. It tasted putrid, but I bit and chewed and swallowed all the same. I needed more; I couldn't stop. I reached for another handful, and somebody tried to push me aside. I elbowed him in the face; his skull collapsed and he fell aside. I didn't care. I took his place, crouching on the ground, and continued to feed on the rancid, putrid flesh and offal.

Eventually the corpse was gone; nothing remained but a few large bones. The small bones had already been snatched up and gnawed. I rejoined the crowd lurching westward. A clump of people were chasing a car. The car was barely moving; it was clearly disabled. The group caught up with it. I ran up and joined in. We smashed at the windows, banged on the doors. Somebody had found a large cinder block, and they now tossed it through the windshield. The glass smashed, and the two people inside screamed. The crowd began rocking the car back and forth. I grabbed a fender and began pushing and pulling, joining in the rocking motion. Back and forth, we pushed and pulled. I looked at the fellow next to me. He only had one arm, and half of his face was missing, yet he pushed and pulled along with the rest of us. The car rocked further and further on each cycle; eventually it tipped up on its side. We scrambled all over it, ripping off the doors and smashing out the windows. Somebody grabbed one of the two occupants, a pretty young woman, and dragged her out. Her legs kicked and her face was a mass of pain and fear. I tried to tell her not to be scared, but no words came from my mouth, only grunts and groans. She screamed and fainted. Soon her head had been ripped off, and we were feasting on her flesh. Another group had dismembered her companion, a young man, and was devouring him with ripping teeth and tearing fingers. Soon they were no more.

Still hungry, I joined back in with the lurching, limping crowd. We hungered, we sought to feed. There was no satiating our need, our lust for flesh. There were more of us than ever; I could see hundreds of us in all directions, all moving westward, overrunning the countryside. To my right was a woman with her chest ripped open. I could see her heart and lungs inside her ruined rib cage. The heart was not beating, but her arms were flailing and her legs were lurching. On my other side was a short fat man. He was bald and missing an ear. His nose was hanging off his face. Both of his eyes were gone. But he lurched and hungered and drooled with the rest of us, needing food.

Off to the side was a small bungalow. A man was standing in the doorway. He saw us, and screamed. His car was thirty feet away from him, and he tried to run to it. Several of us saw our opportunity, and pounced on it. We lurched at top speed toward him. I was closest, and reached him first. He was still ten feet from his car, but he would never reach it now. He threw up his hands, trying to protect his face, but I elbowed him in the side of the head and knocked him down. I stomped on his skull, and heard it crunch. I reached down and grabbed his throat, ripping out his windpipe with my clawing fingers. I brought a fistful of his bloody flesh to my mouth and munched it. It tasted like vomit, but I could not stop feeding. My fellows soon caught up and likewise ripped off bloody chunks of meat from his carcass. Soon he was gone, and we rejoined the migration to the west.

Up ahead was a large house. It was a two-story frame building, and although the windows were boarded up, light still leaked out from the cracks. I caught a glint of metal in an upstairs window, poking out through the boards. It was the barrel of a rifle; it was firing at us. I could see the flash of the gunpowder, could hear the blasts of the bullets. Nobody stopped; we continued toward the house. As I got closer, I saw the barrel spin around toward me. I did not care. I was hungry. The barrel was now pointing directly at me, and it roared again. I felt the bullet go through my chest. I didn't care. Another bullet ripped through my eye socket, removing a chunk of the back of my skull. It hurt like hell, but I didn't care. I continued toward the house. Soon I was pounding on the door along with a dozen of my fellows. A large knife came out through slots in the door, hacking off the fingers and hands of my companions. I lost a few fingers, but I did not stop. Soon we had the door broken down, and we swarmed throughout the house.

Many of us lost more limbs inside the house, but we devoured the half dozen people hiding inside. It didn't matter. We were still starving. We took back to the field, continued lurching toward the sunset in the west. I was missing a hand, an eye, a good sized chunk of my skull, and much of my torso. But it didn't matter. I was so hungry. That's all I knew. I was so very, very hungry.

***

WE WERE A herd now. There were hundreds of us, lurching and limping across the plains, traveling westward, toward the setting sun.

Hundreds of us, lurching mindlessly but now as one, for we had found a leader. I called him "Marvin," but of course I didn't know if that was really his name. None of us could talk. But he gave us purpose, gave us direction, gave us hope. He would wave his arms, scream, and lead us. And we would follow. For we were hungry, so very hungry, and he always led us to food.

Mostly what we hungered for was flesh. Human flesh. Preferably living human flesh, fresh off the bone. We would rip it, shred it, tear it from a still-warm body, devour it hungrily while the last few beats of the heart pumped blood into the dirt, and then move on searching for more. There was no satiating our need, our hunger.

Marvin was relatively intact. He had all four of his limbs, and most of his face. That was more than you could say for most of us, who had many battle scars. I myself was missing an arm and half of my face, not to mention the back of my skull. But Marvin, in his near perfection, gave us all hope. He led us not only to food, but he actually found us places to rest. To rest! I so craved rest, almost as much as food. If only I could feed sufficiently that I might lie down, relax, and rest my bones. Maybe, just maybe, Marvin would make that possible.

Among the hundreds of Marvin's followers were many diverse types. There were young and old, tall and short, fast and slow. Some were strong and hearty, others could barely limp along. But all followed Marvin and trusted his instincts. One follower in particular caught my eye: she was young and vibrant and pretty. She had long blonde hair, bone-white skin, and most of a pretty face. Her eyes were huge and blue. They looked all the more huge for bulging out of their ruined sockets. In my mind, I called her Zelda, though of course I'll never know if that is really her name. Zelda stirred longings in me; longings for a time long past, a time that I can never know again.

We were crossing an open field, heading for a nearby town where there might be people to eat, when a group of soldiers appeared. The military had been deployed to stop our kind and our feeding, and this was one of the patrols. There were maybe twenty of them, all in uniforms and carrying rifles. When they saw us, they went into formation: half lined up and dropped to their knees, rifles raised. The other half stood behind them, rifles also aimed at us. They fired at a command. Bullets ripped through our crowd; of course, nobody cared. A few limbs and skull fragments went flying, but we kept going. We soon overran the soldiers, stomping them to death with our sheer numbers. Another fellow and I picked up one battered soldier from the ground and ripped him in half. I buried my face in his throat, biting and chewing, his blood running down my chin. Others were doing the same with his companions. Soon the soldiers were no more.

We arrived at the town, Marvin roaring in the lead and waving his arms. We were still hungry. There were a few houses, a general store, and a railroad station. Most of the residents were hiding in the station. We fell upon the station and burst through the doors. There were dozens of people huddling inside, but they were no match for our fury. We swarmed and seized them. Five of us would grab one resident and rip him to pieces; then we would shred his carcass and toss chunks of meat to each other. Gore and gristle were everywhere, and the floor was slick. We could barely stand from the coagulating blood and crushed organ meats scattered about. But we gorged on the bright red flesh and organs until we were full. Then we fell to the floor, heedless of the mess, and rested. Zelda was lying near me. I looked at her with my one eye. She looked back. I thought I felt a connection.

When night fell, we were once more on the move. However much we ate, we always hungered again. We crossed the fields, the hundreds of us, grunting and lurching. It was many miles to the next town. Little did we know that we would never make it.

Before long, another deployment of soldiers appeared, but these were better prepared than the last. They came with tanks, armed with cannons. The foot troops carried flamethrowers and wore armor. They had learned. They advanced with confidence, directly into our midst. We took out some of them, but the cannons and flamethrowers were too much for us. Many of my fellows went up in flames, to fall in a charred heap on the ground. Many others were crushed by the tanks, reduced to flat gray pancakes that moved no more. The rest of us scattered, looking for cover. It was the first time I had felt fear in many weeks.

About five of us lurched toward a ravine for cover. As we leapt toward it, several flamethrowers spat out their bright yellow tongues; three of my fellows went up in cinders. I was down to one companion. It was Zelda. I grabbed her around the waist and hurled her into the ravine, rolling out of sight. We came to rest beneath the roots of a giant tree. I held her still, forcing her to stay quiet. We waited, motionless, listening to the battle raging all around us long into the night.

When morning broke, all was quiet. My hunger was worse than ever. I could hide no more. I looked down at Zelda. She was chewing on my leg. I smacked her pretty face with the stump of my arm. She growled at me but pulled her face from my thigh. I poked my head up above the edge of the ravine. Bodies were everywhere, both soldiers and our former companions alike. Our herd had been decimated, the survivors scattered. I pulled Zelda up by her hair. We were alone with the corpses.

We didn't know which way to go. We wandered aimlessly for days, hoping to find our herd, but never did. We hid when tanks and soldiers came by, and waylaid the occasional lone traveler for food. But we were hungrier than ever. I had to smack Zelda several times when she tried to chew on me.

Finally, we spied a large warehouse in the distance. We lurched for it at top speed, hunger raging in our bellies. When we arrived, we found that the doors had already been smashed down. The offices were a mess, riddled with bones and dried gore. We were too late. Our fellows, or another herd, had found this place first and eaten everyone in sight.

I went into the storage area of the warehouse to see what I could find. It was full of crates. Hundreds, maybe thousands of rows of wooden crates, stacked to the ceiling. They were all marked "Spam." I found a crowbar and pried off the lid of the nearest crate. It contained dozens of tins of Spam. They had easy-open pull-off lids, which was fortunate since I didn't have a can opener. I ripped the lid off of a tin, and forced the chunk of pink meat down my throat in a single push, barely bothering to chew or taste. The next three tins went down the same way. Finally, I took the time to chew one, to savor the taste. It was *good!* It tasted much like human flesh, only spicier and less rancid. I could get used to this, I thought.

Zelda was watching me curiously from the doorway, and soon made her way in to the warehouse. I handed her a tin. She pulled it open and gobbled the contents. A smile spread across her pretty half-face. Soon we were sitting cross-legged on the floor of the warehouse, eating tin after tin of the bright pink food. It took us an hour to finish that first crate, and then we lay ourselves down on the floor, side by side, satiated for the first time in weeks.

Knowing that she was no longer hungry and not likely to try to eat me, I pulled Zelda close. She looked deep into my eye. I put my arms around her. Other needs than hunger were now uppermost in our minds. Although neither of us retained a full complement of body parts, we managed to make love before falling back to the floor, satiated once again. She slept.

I got up and explored the warehouse. There was enough Spam here to keep us both fed for at least a hundred years. There was also a small apartment with a living room, a bathroom and a bedroom. The bedroom was spacious, and furnished with a large, comfortable four-poster bed. I went back to the warehouse and brought three crates of Spam into the bedroom. Then I picked Zelda up in my arms, carried her to the apartment, and tossed her onto the mattress. She woke up, looked around, and smiled.

We would be very happy here together.

***

I WAS SPRAWLED on the tar roof of the warehouse on my belly, squinting down the sights of the rifle with my single eye. I lined up one lurching, drooling target, squeezed the trigger, and watched him fall to the ground with his skull shattered. It pained me to kill my own kind, but I had to defend our stronghold. They would gladly overrun us for our wealth of food.

To my left, Antonio squinted along the barrel of his own rifle. He fired twice, and two more of them dropped. I put my eye back to my sights. By the time we were done, the dozen would-be invaders lay in crumpled heaps on the ground.

Antonio jumped to his feet. He was tall and good looking, and still retained most of his appendages. I had found him, wandering aimlessly, on one of my expeditions from the warehouse to search for weapons and supplies. Zelda and I had taken him in to help with the defenses. I had no idea if his name was really Antonio, as neither of us had the power of speech. But he looked like an Antonio to me.

We went down to the yard in front of the warehouse where the crumpled carcasses were sprawled. Antonio and I dragged them to the fire pit and piled them up over a layer of kindling. Soon they were ablaze, and a fine white ash was drifting into the sky. The first few times I had shot invaders, I made the mistake of leaving them on the ground. By morning, they were gone. Apparently our kind cannot be permanently killed, even by a shot to the head. It takes fire to reduce us to our component atoms.

I watched the column of ashes rising into the sky. It almost looked triumphant. This was the first band of invaders we'd seen in quite a while. They seemed to be thinning out. I wondered if that was good news or bad. If the numbers of our kind were dwindling, it could mean that the authorities had figured out how to eliminate us. That would imply that they'd be coming for us soon enough. I should probably have made another trip to the abandoned Wal-Mart where I found the rifles, and see what else I could scrounge up for our defenses.

Back inside our small apartment within the warehouse, Zelda had dinner on the table: a crate of Spam, with an open can on each of our plates. Antonio and I gulped down one can each before even sitting down. Then we settled in and gorged ourselves until we were full. The Spam helped to keep the hunger, the intense and unrelenting hunger for human flesh, at bay. It allowed us to function almost as normal humans. Almost. Zelda ate more daintily, shoveling chunks of Spam into her moist mouth with a battered fork. Her long blonde hair framed her pretty half-face, and her blue eyes stared dreamily at Antonio.

My hunger momentarily sated, I noticed another feeling: jealousy. I hated the way she stared at him. Sure, he was handsome and relatively intact physically, but she was *mine!* I stood up suddenly, knocking my chair backwards, and growled at her. She jerked her head around and regarded me with her usual vacant stare. I grabbed her arm with my one hand and dragged her to the bedroom.

Slamming the door shut, I tossed her onto the bed. She spread her legs wide and I crawled up between them. She tried to bite my shoulder, and I clubbed her with my stump. Clumsily, I made love to her the best I could, given the damaged condition of my genitals and our various missing body parts. It wasn't particularly good for either of us, but I felt the wave of jealousy dissipate.

I left her on the bed, disheveled and half dressed, and went to check on our defenses. I wondered if our next invaders would be more of our own kind, following the scent of Spam, or members of the authorities coming to destroy us. Either way, we had to be ready.

I made my rounds of the warehouse, checking the condition of the bars and boards covering the windows. I checked the locks on all the doors. I checked the pit where we buried the empty Spam cans, attempting to keep any hint of the scent from reaching the ultra-sensitive nostrils of the undead hoards. All seemed to be in order.

Returning to the living quarters, I saw no sign of Zelda. Or of Antonio for that matter. Then I heard it: sounds of grunting and pounding coming from the bedroom. My fist clenched and my stump waving in the air, I burst into the bedroom. He was on top of her, his pelvis gyrating, vigorously giving her what I never could. She stared at me with blank eyes, but her mouth opened and her throat convulsed in soundless, mirthless laughter.

Enraged, I fled the apartment, and ran out the door of the warehouse. I ran, in my lurching, halting gate, without purpose, without thought; with nothing but rage. I lurched past the smoldering remnants of the fire in the pit, and out across the field. I flung myself on the ground and pounded the turf with my fist. I ground my stump into my eye socket, wishing I had the ability to cry.

As I lay there on the turf, I thought for a moment that I could feel my heart pounding. But I knew that was impossible; my heart hadn't beaten for ages. I listened carefully. It was the ground that was shaking. I struggled to my feet and gazed into the distance.

It was a caravan of soldiers. Some were on foot, some on horseback, some in tanks. They were spread out in a line nearly a mile wide, marching across the plain. They were still far off, but if I could see them, they could probably see me. I lurched at top speed back to the warehouse.

Wailing like a banshee, I burst in through the door of the apartment and banged on the furniture to raise the alarm. Antonio and Zelda ran out of the bedroom, zipping up and trying to smooth their ragged clothing. I waved toward the window, toward our advancing attackers.

All three of us fled to the roof this time, each armed with a rifle and several boxes of ammo. There wasn't much hope, but they wouldn't take us without a fight. We sprawled out on the tar surface of the roof, rifles steady and eyes peeled, waiting for the targets to come into range.

I sighted down the barrel. I tried to pick out the leader of the approaching platoon. I squeezed off a shot. It missed by a mile. They were still too far away for our rifles. Unfortunately, they were not too far away for their own weapons. Bullets were soon flying closely over our heads.

I rolled behind an air conditioning compressor for cover. Antonio pulled Zelda behind a chimney. The bastard's hands were all over her. If we got out of this spot, I swore I would shoot and burn him myself.

Antonio poked his head out from behind the chimney and sited his rifle. He squeezed off several rounds in quick succession, none of which hit a target. But a machine gun blast came up from the advancing line of soldiers and ripped his skull in half. He dropped to the tar surface of the roof, his brains spilling out in a great gray mess.

Zelda ran to him, wailing in pain and fear. The half-moon of her face was twisted nearly beyond recognition. Then she ran toward the front edge of the roof, hysterical. Machine gun fire riddled her body from several locations. She fell in a sprawled mess, her skull shattered and her limbs nearly severed from her torso.

It was up to me now. If I could repel the troops, maybe I could patch her back together. But Antonio would go right to the bonfire. My face grim, I threw myself down and crawled, army-style, toward the front edge of the roof, maintaining as low a profile as possible. Bullets whirred about my ears like bumblebees. The troops were close now, so very close. I could smell their flesh; I longed to eat it. I shot round after round; some scored hits, and a few soldiers dropped. But most of my rounds bounced harmlessly off body armor. Still the troops came. They were nearly upon the warehouse by now. I focused on the leader again, astride a huge horse. I would take him out, and then they would be in disarray.

There was a sound behind me. I whipped my neck around, and there was a soldier standing at the far side of the roof. The sneaky bastard had circled around the building and climbed up. I rose to my knees. He raised his pistol and pointed at my head. He squeezed.

I didn't feel the bullet as it ripped through my skull. I could barely feel anything these days. But I lost all control of my motor functions, and fell to the tar. I couldn't move a muscle. I lay there as more troops climbed to the roof. I heard them talking, orders being barked.

Zelda, Antonio and I were unceremoniously tossed off the roof to the ground. One of the troops produced an axe and proceeded to hack our limbs off our bodies, and to sever our heads. It didn't hurt. Our parts were tossed into the fire pit, on top of some broken-up pallets. Fortunately, my head came to rest with my eye facing Zelda's head. I stared hard at her, to see if she retained any consciousness. I couldn't tell.

They splashed gasoline over us, and a soldier came up with a flamethrower. I wondered if burning would hurt. I was guessing not. The tongue of flames licked out, and we were ablaze. I was wrong about the burning; it hurt like the Dickens. I rolled my eye toward Zelda. I thought I saw her eye twitch a little. *She still loves me!* My consciousness was ebbing, but I managed to hang on to one final thought as the blanket of oblivion took me: *Zelda! I will love you always!*

Epilogue:

The column of white ash rose slowly into the sky, and arced lazily over the countryside. Eventually, it was absorbed into a fluffy white cloud that happened to be drifting by, the small ash particles binding with the water vapor. The cloud drifted on the breeze, and was soon miles away.

Days later, the cloud encountered a sudden low pressure system, which dropped the ambient temperature below the dew point. This occurred directly over the water reservoir of the tiny town of Rock Ridge. The water vapor condensed, and thousands of tiny raindrops fell earthward, splashing to the water's surface to create a beautiful network of ripples, spreading in ever expanding circles as they merged gently with the town's drinking water supply.

HUNGRY

JENNIFER WORD

MY NAME IS William B. Hensfield. I am a retired lawyer of the California court of appeals. Yes, I used to work as an Appelate Attorney for the 4th District Court of Appeal, in Division One, located in San Diego which holds jurisdiction over matters from Imperial and San Diego Counties.

I was born in 1979. In 2001, I graduated and moved on to Law School. I was twenty-one then. When I was twenty-five, I passed the California Bar and went to work as an associate in the Law Firm of Weston, Beals and Oremor. That was in 2005.

Eight years later, in November of 2013, I was emergency sworn in as a commissioner of civil marriages. It was simply a formality. I was thirty-three. A year earlier, my wife had just given birth to our first child, a son, that we named Jackson.

Jackson Hensfield was born on October 12, 2012, and died on October 13. On October 15, during the funeral, little Jackson began to cry. At first, everyone thought it was the wind. It was low and muffled. Although, the day was bright and sunny (such a juxtaposition to the mood), and thinking there might be wind whistling through the oaks of the cemetery really made no sense. But still, several people later told me that they all thought that's what it was at first, too.

Until everyone heard the light pounding coming from inside the tiny coffin. I never knew they made coffins that small until little Jackson passed away. He didn't stay inside for very long. Melissa (that's my wife, or should I say 'was') became frantic.

"He didn't die! Jackson is alive!! They made a mistake!! He's *hungry!*"

Her words will forever haunt me. Jackson was *hungry* all right; but he wasn't alive. Not in the true medical sense. October 15, 2012, is when it all started.

No one knew then, and they still don't know today, what caused it, or why some were affected and others weren't. It's worldwide. I only write this down now, because future generations may not understand this. Sure, it will be in all the history books, but that won't explain the *experience*.

Imagine: not knowing if *you* will become one of them. A bus could hit you, or that nasty smoking habit could catch up, or you could get into a lethal barroom fight while defending your girl. Next thing you know? You've got a serial walking impediment, you're socially ostracized and your penchant for chewing on human flesh rages out of control.

It isn't like all those old movies said it would be. Romero only got part of it right. Zombies *are* real. They *do* like to eat human flesh, and their rotting bodies are a serious hindrance to societal functioning. However, once reanimated (in that mystery way that no one can seem to explain), they can still think, sometimes talk—at least until their teeth fall out and their tongues rot away—and even work.

It sucks; plain and simple. America just got a whole new set of social challenges heaped upon it. Some of the ones that come back (especially drowning victims) don't even look all that gruesome. Some people are happy their loved ones come back, while others are horrified (rightfully so). Some get jealous when their loved ones don't return knocking on their doors, while their neighbors get half the family plot showing up. You just never know what you're going to get.

And some people have had to deal with real heartache. Like a newborn (stillborn) coming back to life in its tiny coffin at the flippin' funeral.

Melissa went a little nuts. She was never the same after. When the coffin was opened up, little Jackson had been dead and decomposing for a couple of days. Plus, he'd been dead inside the womb for over a week, even though we hadn't known. We just thought Mel was going into labor a couple of weeks early, we had no clue Jackson had died with the umbilical cord tangled around his neck; Mel's body was trying to flush out the dead fetus.

Jackson was a nightmare. And before anyone could stop him, the officiating Priest had grabbed a stick lying on the ground, and thrust it through the little soft spot that all newborns have. Jackson died again on October 15, 2012. This time, he stayed that way.

That was just the beginning. Six years later, and the legal battles rage on. Those that had a spouse who died and came back, sometimes wanted to stay married and deal with the hassles. True love. California surprised the entire country by becoming the first state to recognize human-zombie marriages.

Of course, we didn't legalize zombie marriage. But, for those human couples who were already married, and one person just happened to die and come back, we created special laws for 'recognizing' those unions as still valid. It appeased the majority of the left wing, and the right wing could accept that. Thank goodness.

That's where I come in. I was emergency sworn in as a commissioner of civil marriages, remember? As a formality, I already stated. I never imagined when I went to Law School that this would end up being my career. I was emergency sworn in and then sworn in again, in a new position created in conjunction with the amended California Marriage Laws.

My official title is a Solemnization Consummation Authority. S.C.A. God, what a job. You see, for those couples that find themselves zombifically challenged, it's my job to bear witness to certain, ahem, 'acts'. Personally, I think the California Supreme Court Justices are a bunch of perverts. But the damn laws passed, and my commission was created. It pays well, too, let me tell you.

What do I do? Well, as a Solemnization Consummation Authority, a.k.a. agent, I preside over the final decree that a human-zombie marriage is, in fact, valid. California decided that any human-zombie couples who wanted to remain together and married, could do so, provided they could supply proof of consummation of the marriage post-zombification. It's a crazy world we live in.

Solemnization simply means: To celebrate or observe with dignity and gravity; or to perform with formal ceremony. It's my job to observe the successful consummation of a human-zombie union. If the couple in question cannot perform the deed, their marriage will be annulled. They get three chances to successfully perform this act in my presence, otherwise, no dice.

I know, I know, you're probably curious. I get asked these

questions all the time; from friends, family, and curious party-goers at random shindigs and gatherings. The most common question I get asked is: What constitutes 'successful' completion of the act? Does the zombie in question have to reach climax?

The laws spell it all out in detail, and they've been quite fair. No, the zombie in question does not have to reach a climax. Male zombies don't always produce enough 'liquid' to pull off successful ejaculation. However, some continue to produce live sperm, if you can believe that. And yes, there have been some human-zombie pregnancies (most end in miscarriage) and even a few zombabies born. Most of those die within a few days, but again, everything is so random.

The news occasionally reports (with freak enthusiasm every time) about a human baby miraculously born from a zombie father.

It's always a zombie father, however, since, for some reason, male zombies can still manufacture sperm, but female zombies seem to lose all their reproductive capabilities. Medicine (as usual) can't figure this out, either. Maybe all the eggs dry up and die?

Climax is not required. Especially since females, classically, don't reach climax during intercourse nearly as often as men do, and if it's a female zombie in question, that wouldn't be fair, now would it? I'm told that female zombies almost never reach orgasm. Sucks for them.

So, no, I answer people when they ask, zombies don't have to reach a climax. They simply have to successfully perform intercourse; meaning—a penis (whether human or zombie at this point) has to enter a vagina (again, human or zombie) and, well . . . everyone knows how that works. The couple in question can move around for however long they want. There's no specification on how long things have to last. And, again, no climax is required.

The challenge for the majority of these couples is simply in the logistics of the act. First off, zombies want to eat human flesh. Cow's brains and pig's feet will do the job, but, they still want to eat people, it's their top choice. And even though these 'people' can still talk and 'reason', their deep urge to cannibalize leaves them struggling with great difficulty to not eat even their most cherished loved ones.

They work, too, but in shackles . . . like morbid chain gangs, cleaning up garbage along busy highways and recreational parks. They wear muzzles. Zombie suicide is prevalent. Who would want to live that way? But some do. And many want to remain married and have it recognized by the courts. There are significant tax breaks to being married to a zombie.

So, my job, as unbelievable as it is, is to go to these people's houses, on official business, and witness their sexual act. I can't believe this is what I do.

It would seem like some sick, twisted fetish, wouldn't it? Trust me, the Zombie Porn industry is bursting, no pun intended. I can't believe how many sick perverts actually get off on watching this stuff. Me? I don't get off on it. It's just my job, remember?

Mel had a hard time dealing with it. After Jackson, and the associations, I don't blame her. But the money was too good to pass up. She refused to get pregnant again. She was too terrified the baby would die in utero, and I knew she wouldn't remain sane if she had to go through that even one more time. It was too much of a risk.

We talked about adopting as well, but . . . since no one knows who might or might not live or die, again, she couldn't deal with it. What if the little tyke contracted childhood leukemia, or got hit by a car, but didn't stay dead? Mel didn't want any zombie kids running around, muzzled inside our house.

Truthfully, I think what freaked her out the most about my new job, was the thought that it could happen to us. I've often wondered what she would have done if I had died and come back. Would she have stayed with me? Would she have loved me enough to visit the courts, pay those fees and fill out the paperwork? Would she have been willing to have an S.C.A. agent watch us have sex? Because that, folks, is true love right there.

A lot of people say the whole thing is just sick and wrong. Other die-hard romantics swoon and say it's . . . well, romantic. I'm on the fence. I watch zombie sex acts (and attempts) all week long, so the shine and allure of romance often dulls. I try to keep an open mind, however. I mean, whatever goes on behind closed bedroom doors is really no one's business. Except for me, it is. It's my business.

It didn't affect me at first; the first few times I watched it. Often times, the couple asks me for help or advice. I'm allowed to talk them through it, and even 'coach' them a bit, but I can't physically intervene. I sit in a chair, next to the bed.

Let me explain a common scenario. We'll do, say, human male vs. zombie female, okay? That one is actually much more common.

Husbands seem to want to keep their zombie wives around much more often than female wives want a zombie-husband. It makes sense.

So, I come into these homes, and typically, the wife is tied or handcuffed to the bed posts. Her feet are usually tied as well, and she's muzzled, so she can't bite her lover's neck out. Sometimes she has a bag over her head as well; I presume because she's rotting in the face too much to want to look at.

The room is usually heavily laden with perfume, Febreze, or burning scented candles. It often smells very pleasant, actually, with a bit of sickly-rotten fruit smell, just underneath.

Sometimes it takes the husband a bit of time to 'get excited'. Other times, it doesn't take any time at all. You can see their excitement poking through their pants. Some of them actually seem to get off on having a witness.

Anyhow, as I was saying, the common scenario with a husband vs. a zombie wife is simply that he gets naked (she is always already naked and tied up before I get there), he climbs on top of her, and they do it. It usually doesn't take very long, as the male is almost always very excited. In these cases, climax is a definite.

I mark it down on my clipboard (among many other notes) and check off the successful completion box. Wham, Bam and Done. Again, no pun intended.

When it gets a bit more complicated is when it's a zombie husband vs. a human wife. Again, when I come in, they are already tied up. This is a specification before I show up on an appointment. The S.C.A. agent is never supposed to be put into any situation where they might be in danger of an attack. There are heavy fines if I show up at a residence and the zombie is not already contained. Before the appointment, of course, we get the zombies' agreement to events, so don't go thinking this is all happening against their will or anything.

If they are capable, they sign a consent form. If they are able, they verbally consent. This all happens at a special set of offices downtown. It's the human spouse's responsibility to safely transport their beloved zombie significant other to the premises, shackled and muzzled, in order to fill out this paperwork. Like I said, it takes dedication. The courts figure that anyone willing to go to that much trouble must really be doing it out of love. But I digress.

When I enter the bedroom, the male is tied up (usually with chains, since male zombies are stronger), and he's naked. So is the woman. Modesty seems to fly out the window in most of these cases. I've only had a few wives be shy, and they simply removed their underwear, while wearing long skirts that they hiked up.

Anyway, the problem with a male zombie is that they don't always get excited. The husbands can simply lube up with their zombie wives, and there's no problem there. But with a zombie husband, sometimes a little creativity is called for.

Zombie men become aroused by blood. So, if the zombie husband isn't already sporting a boner, the wife will often times need to dangle a raw steak over his face, or some animal brains, or a pint of pig's blood. When this happens, it's like watching a tent being pitched.

Then the wife climbs on board and does her thing, dangling the raw and bloody morsels in front of their husband's face the entire time. Sometimes they suspend the meat from the ceiling on a hook, so they can keep their hands free to touch themselves. But, again, climax isn't required. As long as successful arousal and penetration occurs, the marriage is deemed official.

They only have to do it once. As soon as I check off that box, they're married for life. Or unlife, as it were. Whatever problems will arise for those couples from that point on—that's their business. The divorce courts have their own new laws for dealing with human-zombie splits. Again, no pun intended.

I don't care about that. I only care about my part of the job. A lot of people tell me I'm the luckiest guy in the world. I get paid to watch sex all week long. And no matter how smelly, foul, disgusting or gruesome it might be, they all say it still beats the nine-to-five grind in some corner cubicle farm. I suppose they're right.

But if that's the case, why is it so hard to keep the numbers in my position? They keep raising the incentives, increasing the salaries and bonuses with every year an S.C.A. agent stays on board. If it's such a great job, why is the turnover rate so high?

Yes, I know, it messes with your personal life. My wife had a serious problem with it. She was embarrassed to tell any of our family or friends at first. I couldn't hide it forever, though. And I've seen the scared look on people's faces when they find out what I do.

A lot of them are curious and ask questions, but many others simply disappear to the other side of the room. Even the ones that ask the questions quickly lose interest, once I begin to relay the gory details. The ones who don't leave and remain interested are the people who scare me the most. They get this greedy-wet look in their eyes, like they wish *they* were in *my* position. As if they think they would appreciate it more than me. I can tell these are the types of people who would need to excuse themselves after every appointment to go whack off in the bathroom.

And in case any sick perverts are wondering, of course, as an S.C.A. agent, I have strict guidelines I must follow. If I do get excited while watching an 'act', I'm not allowed to touch myself. I certainly can't masturbate in front of the clients. Masturbation, even in private, has to be done away from the client's residence. I'm not even allowed to do it in their bathroom. No masturbation is allowed on the premises, and that includes in my car, parked in their driveway.

It's a respectful job, with as much tact and aplomb as is possible, under the circumstances. No one is made to feel dirty or ashamed. It's simply a formality.

But there are drawbacks. Like I said, the social ostracizing is difficult. It's gotten to the point where I don't tell people what I do anymore, or I lie. And it does mess with your head a bit.

Mel tried to tell me that once, but I told her she was full of shit. I mean, after Jackson, we weren't exactly doing it, you know? Her hormones were all messed up, not to mention her head. Plus there was this crazy zombie shit all over the news. It went on for weeks, months. Then the world had to deal with it and adjust.

New laws were passed, new organizations, support groups sprang up. New industries were born. Zombie-porn, specialty butcher shops, a whole new branch of social services, etc. Special court buildings had to be constructed, new registration offices opened to deal with incorporating back into the system those who were legally declared dead, but were now walking around again. Special schools were opened to try and help those zombies who'd lost the ability of speech. Fucking zombie-sign language. Someone invented that.

People have gotten rich off this catastrophe. Others have been devastated. I got a job out of it, with a really nice pension package and a whole new set of issues in my fucked up brain.

Yeah, Mel tried to tell me once that the job was messing with my head. She said it was 'changing' me. Eventually she couldn't deal with it. She left a few years back. I was too numb at that point to care. If I did feel anything, it was anger. Fuck her for leaving. I'm the one that has to deal with this shit every week; every day, in fact.

I mean, so what if after a few months of this job, I couldn't get it up anymore? So fucking what? And who cares if I got desperate to sport a woody, and figured out that watching that stupid zombie-porn was the only thing that worked?

I never asked Mel to watch it with me. I told her I could just watch it for a few minutes downstairs alone, then come into the bedroom and please her. She told me I was sick and demented, however. She asked me if I thought those zombie-girls were hotter than her. Pff.

I mean, to her credit, she did try a bit. At one point, she did get really drunk and smear herself with some bloody juice from some raw steaks in the fridge. Before that, she'd tried fake blood from this Halloween costume kit, but it smelled like sugar, and that's not what zombies smell like.

So what if I started needing a few rotting pieces of day old, rancid meat to be kept in the room? The smell just seemed to help with my arousal time, that's all. It was no big deal. I don't know why she freaked out and left, I really don't.

So what if I once asked her if I could tie up her arms and legs and put a bag over her head? I don't know why she got so upset that one time I tried to suspend a cow brain from the ceiling. It was kinky. You'd think she'd be willing to be a little more open-minded. Couples have to work at this stuff, you know? It's difficult.

But she left. It's okay, though. I'm fine. I'm perfectly healthy.

I've seen my therapist. I had one specifically assigned to me for the job. How 'bout that? Every S.C.A. agent gets their very own, personal shrink. He tells me there's nothing wrong with me. He says my reactions are perfectly normal, given the situation. He says my job has to come home with me, and that this is one of those cases where work simply will bleed into your personal life.

They tell you not to take it home with you, but in this case, that type of removed categorization would be the unhealthy thing to do, my doctor assures me. The fact that it is affecting my personal life is a good thing, he says.

He really seems to enjoy hearing about my job. The appointments, he asks for lots of details, tells me it's healthy to talk about it all. Everything is confidential, of course. And it's his job to listen, but I really do feel as if he's not just doing a job, he truly cares. He likes to hear about every appointment I go to, so I know he's not just checking out during our sessions. He's a really good therapist. He takes tons of notes. I'm a really lucky guy.

So, my therapist says I'm just fine. Some people simply don't have what it takes to stomach what I do. I'm sure I'll find a new wife at some point. First I need to secure a girlfriend.

I had one, briefly. I lied to her and didn't tell her what I do. I just said I work for the courts. I have a lot of money, so she didn't seem to care beyond the basic explanation. But she seemed to take offense at some of my sexual preferences. When she finally broke up with me, she told me I had an 'unhealthy fetish' and that I should go see someone. She told me I needed professional psychiatric help.

I would have told her I already had that, and that my doctor tells me I'm totally normal, but she ran out of my apartment too fast. I really don't know why she freaked out, just because I told her I wanted to have someone sit in a chair and watch us do it. That's not so weird. Lots of people are into voyeurism.

But, whatever; as my shrink says, I'm perfectly normal. He says I just need to find someone who's a good match for me. I need to find someone who is into what I'm into—someone with the same tastes as me.

A lot of new industries popped up with the zombies. This whole thing has really changed the world. As I've said, the butcher's shops, the courts, the schools, the pornos. Not all zombies who come back were married, either. And not all of them want to work the chain gangs picking up garbage. And with all those pornos being made, there's a new industry in the escort business as well.

Pimps got in on the action, just like everybody else. Where there's money to be made, people will flock. And zombies need to make a living, too.

My shrink says it's perfectly normal. Everyone has their specific tastes, and no one can judge or say what is right or wrong in the areas of sexual preference. I mean, it makes sense.

Shrinks are supposed to remain objective. He can't anymore tell me I'm sick or perverted for my 'fetish' as my ex-wife called it, than he could if I was attracted to other men, or wanted to engage in S&M. There's no judgment in that guy's office. As long as I'm willing to talk about it all, not hide it, share the juicy details, he tells me I'm totally normal.

So, my wife left me, and so did my girlfriend. My one and only son was a newborn zombie. No biggie.

I have a really good psychiatrist, and a cushy, secure job as an S.C.A. agent. All-in-all, I'd say my life is going pretty well. But I am a human male, and men have their needs. No one seems to be willing to help me out with these things.

I have plenty of money, and there's nothing wrong with me. I do my job, and occasionally I need physical release. Fuck having a girlfriend or wife. Clearly, these human women can't understand my needs.

But I know a place to go.

I know I can find a woman who won't have any trouble being tied up, or having a raw cow brain hung in front of her face. In fact, I know a place where there are girls who will buck and thrash even harder from that.

A little blood dripping onto their face?

That will only make them *more* excited. And that's what I want. It's what I need. I want them excited. I want them *hungry*. Hungry for *me*.

The thing my ex-wife and my stupid ex-girlfriend could never understand is that I need a woman who truly acts as if she *wants* me. These zombies, sure, they want to eat people, but the thing is, they *want* people. I get it now, why these married couples want to stay together. I get why the human spouse wants to stay married to their zombie partner. They come back from the dead, and they *want* their living spouse in a whole new way they never did before.

Being wanted that way, it really does make a person feel loved and desired. In love stories and erotic poems, scribes always talk about the *longing* of love—the *voracious appetite of attraction. The lusty hunger and the desire for flesh.*

In my opinion, zombies are the epitome of human desire. They are the ultimate answer to everything. That's probably why all of this happened. People need to stop being so uptight and embrace the beauty of what's happened to our world. I have.

I know now what I need. And I know where to go to get it. I love my job, and I also love myself. Tonight, I'm going to love something new. Tonight, for the very first time, I'm going to feel what it's like to truly be wanted by another being that is *hungry* for me.

I am an S.C.A. agent. This is what I do, but it's not who I am. I just have certain needs now. My name is William B. Hensfield. I am a retired lawyer of the California court of appeals, and I couldn't be more happy about that.

ALMOST ZOMBIE

BRUCE MEMBLATT

I FOUND HIM in the street, shaggy, befuddled and the answer to my prayers. He turned me into a zombie. He fucked me over with his sassy smile and his bohemian ways.

I didn't know I wanted to be a zombie until I found myself doing the really cool stuff, like eating the flesh off of the cheerleaders at school, or scaring the shit out of the cops. Anyway, his name is Brandon, just plain Brandon, no middle or last, like Beyonce. I call him Bran. All the other girls call him Z. Guess why? But we're tight, like special, we share secrets. My name is Becky. Yeah, I know you're going to say Becky and Brandon, how cute—but it isn't like that, it's never cute. It's hot like blood and flesh. It's bad. *We* are bad. He stays in my room. My parents haven't found out. Good thing, because if they did Bran would make me eat their flesh, and I would. I would do anything for Bran, anything, like tonight.

Tonight we took out a 7-11. We *had* to. We had the munchies. We got high with Brenda and Jim out on the field near the high school, the one with all the willow trees. I've known Brenda since third grade. We've been through everything together. I even know what she needs a boy to do to make her climax. Brenda is really hooked on Jim, but I think she has the hots for Bran.

Everyone has the hots for Bran, and not just because he's a zombie. It's not like they're frightened of him. They love him, even the guys. Bran is awesome in the truest sense of the word. But tonight the stakes were high. The old couple that ran the 7-11 threatened Bran. Can you believe that? Threatened to call the cops. Well, screw them. We ate 'em before you could say 'jeepers creepers'. The thing was they had a gun pointed at me. But Bran didn't care. Jim peed in his pants—and Brenda? Well, she just about fainted on the floor. But that old couple satisfied our munchies fine.

Bran says it's because he loves us. That one day soon we'll consume the whole town, eat all the adults, and then he's going to make us zombies just like him. Not like the ones we are now—partials—but zombies all the time; the bomb. It will be a real party town. I told him, everyone but my parents and I mean it.

He's not like the zombies you read about. He's beautiful. He's got the palest crunchy skin and eyes that sizzle like electricity. He *is* electric. His teeth are like fangs. We'll have teeth like that too, electric eyes and teeth that rip.

I've been trying to ease my parents into it gently, getting them prepared to move. If they don't they'll be munchies, too. They tell me I'm crazy or taking drugs or both, but I have to get them out.

My mom had just left the kitchen. I saw her in the hall. She's always in the kitchen, it seems, or making her way to the kitchen.

So I said, "Hey, Mom."

And she said, "What, Becky?"

She always says 'What, Becky?' with exhaustion in her voice. I don't know why.

And I said, "Mom, it's almost time. You and Dad have to find a new place to live."

So she responded, "Becky, enough. Do you want to see a therapist?"

"I don't need a therapist. Listen, if you guys don't get out soon you'll be toast."

Then she began to scream, "Becky, knock it off!"

So, I just ran back into my room. Bran was in the bed rolling a joint, amused at his own excess. There was some story on the TV about people disappearing; same old story they ran every day. What a drag.

But Bran didn't look like a zombie lying on the bed, he looked like an ordinary kid just getting high. I told him so. I also told him we'd have to do something to get my parents out of town.

He turned to me and said, "Forget about it. They're not your parents anymore."

And for a moment I almost believed him.

Bran didn't say much, so when he did say something it sounded important, like it could be written on a tablet in stone.

Then I said, "Why can't they stay here, alive—isn't it up to you?"

"The plan can't be changed," he said, calm as a breeze, and he took another drag off the joint.

That's when I remember thinking Bran had a flaw. That he was too rigid, like conservative, and I thought I'd have to work on him too. I had my hands full. Then I could hear my mom downstairs yelling something about how the neighborhood was changing, and I thought *if she only knew . . .*

My hair. I had been meaning to wash my hair. That was just a random thought that crossed my mind when I was thinking of what to say to Bran. I'd needed a plan too.

I pulled my shirt off, to get his attention, and I said, "Why don't we scare them, scare them enough to make them run?"

He glared at me. "They'll never leave without you. Put your shirt back on. We're going out."

"Out where?"

"To jam. Just one more day and it begins."

The way he said it made me melt. Like I said, he was bad. *We* were bad.

I only had one more day.

That night, at the field near the high school, all the kids gathered. There must have been hundreds of them, giggling, acting cool. The place was alive, and Bran almost looked alive too. There was chanting, and fire and order. Bran called them to order and I thought about order. The way Bran controlled them made me think of assembly at the high school just above the hill. Was there a difference? Like that old song goes: meet the new boss, same as the old boss. I craved chaos. I thought Bran would bring chaos. Still, he was so fine, like a *god* that night. He tossed me a branch he'd made into a torch. We loved fire. I was at his side like a jungle queen. And he began to speak.

He moved his hands with the breeze. They watched, silent, like they were at a concert and the band had suddenly become still. He said, "Tomorrow we rise."

Then he said the word 'rise' over and over and they repeated it. *Rise. Rise. Rise . . .* Like in a church, only we were outside under the moon. It was awesome. *Bran* was awesome. I think they would have done anything he said, like if he told them to kill me, they would have, but they weren't going to kill me.

Although we *were* going to kill all the adults in town, every last one of them. It was going to be a blast. Munchie fever. If it weren't for my parents, I thought, how it always came down to my parents. Maybe Bran was right. Maybe they weren't my parents anymore? Shit, I thought about everything.

Bran continued to speak and they kept eating it up. As he spoke, I caught Brenda's eye. She was up front, in the first row, standing next to Jim. Jim looked like he was in a trance. They all looked fucked up. I winked at Brenda in the way I did when I needed her to follow me. Then I turned and I told Bran I'd be right back. He was so caught up in the crowd and in his words he didn't even notice I'd left.

Brenda followed me to the tree by the entrance to the high school. We could still hear the chanting in the background. We could see the torches burning.

We leaned against the tree. "What's up?" she said, cracking her gum. Brenda always had a piece of gum in her mouth.

I said, "I have a plan to get my parents out."

She said, "Shit, not that again."

And I said, "Brenda listen."

Then she snapped. "Why are you so stuck on your parents? I can't *stand* mine. Can't wait 'til they're veal."

"Veal?" I said, and then I told her, "Listen, if my parents see this they might actually believe me. Help me bring them back here. *Now,* before it's too late."

I didn't think she'd agree so easily, but she did. Brenda is a true friend even if she is out there. Don't tell her I said that. Anyway, we headed toward my house. We ran.

We reached my door. We could see the lights in the living room. Every night the same thing. The two of them parked in front of the TV. My mom running back and forth fetching snacks—*like zombies,* I thought, and grinned inside.

I turned the key in the latch. When Mom saw the look on Brenda's face she knew something was up. My dad just sighed. Dad sighs a lot. I looked at both of them and I said it urgently. I didn't know what I was going to say at first. I just had to make them come.

And then it came to me. "Mom, Dad, there's a fire by the school—you have to come!"

Brenda looked cross-eyed at me, but she shook her head in agreement.

My mom looked up at me from the couch and said, "Why? Are we the fire department?"

Mom always answers everything with a question.

Then, I just got real frustrated and I screeched, "*Pleeeeeeeeeese.*"

Brenda kept shaking her head. My dad stood up and grabbed my mother's hand like he was suddenly the boss when everyone knew Mom was always in charge. But for some reason she let him be in charge that night. Mom and Dad have a lot of issues, but they're mostly okay. I mean, I wouldn't mind having a relationship like theirs if this thing with Bran doesn't work out. But there was time. I hoped.

As we approached the school, I don't have to tell you, all bets were off. Mom saw right away that there was no fire, of course, and Dad about a second later. Brenda kept pointing like there was a fire. I told her she could stop.

She cracked her gum, kicked the gravel road with her foot, turned to my mother and said, "I'm sorry, Becky made me . . . ."

That's when I leered at her. I was just about to explain everything to Mom and Dad, when they heard the chanting, and caught the light from the torches in their eyes. I was relieved. I guess I had, shall we say, a lack of credibility with my parents at that moment. My credibility would unfortunately soon be recovered.

Becky took off and ran toward Jim. Mom and Dad watched her. I told them about Bran, about being a zombie, a partial, and how the whole town was going to turn around. Mom still didn't believe me.

She looked at me and said, "Becky, they're all just a bunch of drugged up kids."

That's when Dad got angry and grabbed my hand, like he was going to pull me out of there. Like he could save me, save us, like I wanted saving. They didn't understand. It was right in front of their eyes and they still didn't get it. I wanted to scream. I almost did, when we saw the torches coming closer.

Bran was in front leading them. The chanting got louder. He saw me standing with my parents and he glared at me. "Get her!"

I turned around. I pled with Mom and Dad, "Run, just run!"

They wouldn't listen. Mom just looked at me like I was insane.

Dad sighed and hollered, "We're calling their parents. All of them!'

I screamed, "Look at them, look at Bran, at his eyes, at his skin, at his teeth."

And then we were surrounded. I could feel the heat from the torches. I could see their electric eyes everywhere. The moon was so full and bright. I could feel my parents shake. Their breaths getting heavy, so heavy they couldn't speak. I saw Bran and his minions hovering near them. The damn chanting wouldn't stop. Then they fell. I could hear crunching; the unearthly sound of my parents being devoured. Then Bran's face suddenly shot up and he stared at me. I saw the blood, their blood dripping from his mouth. He laughed. They all laughed. He came toward me. I was so taken with him. Taken with the blood, I swooned.

There are songs for all different occasions, but I don't know if there was a song for this one. I was a partial, I still loved my parents, I tried to get them out, but I couldn't feel the pain I should have felt. I *normally* would have felt. I was on my way to becoming a full zombie. I couldn't cry.

Then right by my feet I spotted this big stake and I thought, hey you never know. I was shoving in my bag when I saw Bran coming.

He grabbed me and pulled me toward his side. He raised his arms and shouted to the crowd, to me, to the sky, "It begins now!"

He stretched his hand, and they began to march toward town. Hundreds of them heading down the road. Their eyes gleaming, their teeth eager. The town wouldn't know what hit it. By tomorrow night all would be consumed. We'd be free. *Free.*

Their chants grew softer as they headed into the distance. Bran and I stood behind, by the tree, and we watched. My parents' remains lay by our feet.

He stared at me and said, "We'll join them later for the feast. First, take me back to the house."

I was happy. I thought we were going to make some ritualistic-kind of voodoo victory love. It was going to be hot. Hot like flesh and blood.

The moon watched over us on the walk back to the house. There were screams in the distance.

When we opened the door, he pulled me inside and swept me up to my room. I was ready, ready for the heat. He threw me on the bed. He pawed at me. I was growing wild. He was on top of me. He held my hands down.

He softly whispered, "When they're finished, I'll eat them one by one. That's the plan. That's always been the plan."

And then I plunged that stake I found right through his zombie brain.

Poor Bran didn't know what hit him.

KISSING COUSINS

KEVIN McCLINTOCK

"SHE'S A MIGHTY cute one, that one there," Billy Bowers said, looking over the woman that couldn't have been more than a day over eighteen. "Nice titties and—*Jesus!* Look at that ass!"

Bobby Bowers, Billy's deafmute cousin, looked the girl over and certainly liked what he saw. He glanced over at his cousin, nodded, and then "talked" in his wordless whimpering of his—a bit of drool bubbling from the corner of his mouth.

Despite the contrary, Bobby wasn't retarded. In fact, his collective IQ was much higher than that of his cousin's. He just couldn't hear. And he was physically repulsive to look at—born, as he was, without a voice box, left nipple and right eye. It's why most people thought of him as weak in the brains. Truth be told, he was rather weak in the knees, for he let his older cousin by three years, Billy, boss him about. Especially now, after his dear Papa had died to the zombies and his stepmother raped by a gang of lesbian bikers out searching for "a piece of ass." Bobby had taken him under his wing, so to speak, and had let him onto his post-zombie job.

Herding zombies.

"You ready, pilgrim?" Billy asked.

Bobby read his cousin's lips, enthusiastically nodding.

"Okay then. Grab that cow leg and let's get a move on."

The two men left the yawning doorway of the two-story barn and made their way down a worn, dirt path toward a distant, dusty corral. Various shapes moved inside. The stench, even with winds blowing away to the west, was rising rapidly to unbearable levels.

"Did you bleed them last night, Bobby? Like I asked you to?"

"Swefnesssssss," his cousin slurred.

"Goddammit Bobby. Now they'll be all hungry and pissed off!"

The giant, Bobby, hung his head like a kicked mutt. He stalked ahead to unlatch the metal gate and swing it open. Approaching, Billy unslung his heavy .450 Weatherby rifle, chambering a round. Sliding hunting shades down over his eyes, he nodded to his one-eyed cousin to rope off the girl they'd named Gary.

"The one we picked and named," he instructed, even gesturing out to her. They'd long run out of girl names, so now they were giving the chosen ones guy's names. "Go ahead..."

Stacked atop each other near the inner gate were a bunch of rusty cages. Inside were a number of shivering, mortified animals. Mostly discarded pets, left behind by their dead owners. There were three dogs, five cats, a couple of chickens and a huge rat the Bower cousins had dubbed 'Ben.'

Smelling Bobby now, the eight zombies locked inside the horse corral began scrambling to reach him, growls filling the air. Some fell into the mud as their pals struggled to reach Bobby first. As the group neared him, he began unlatching the animal's cages – two dogs, a cat and a chicken.

Terrified, and nearing a frenzied hysteria that always made the two men guffaw, the animals burst free from their cages, dropping two feet to the pen's muddy ground and scrambling to escape the charging zombies.

Seeing the movement and smelling the blood coursing through the animal's bodies, most of the deadheads forgot about Bobby and zeroed in on the terrified animals instead. Here, the pack broke up into smaller groups as they chased the animals around in the dust.

Over by the perimeter fence, Billy gestured toward his cousin. "C'mon Bob... let's get the bitch isolated!"

He'd climbed on the steel-meshed fence and now held his precious rifle in both arms, an amused look stitched across his face.

But what he'd ordered his cousin to do was easier said than done.

One of the dogs—a small Terrier—let out a screech you wouldn't think a tiny dog of that size could make. A female zombie had fallen on it, her weight breaking the animal's hindquarters. The canine snapped at the hands that, moments later, crushed its skull. Along the east fence, a chicken squawked as it was caught.

Bobby giggled. He loved the sounds those chickens made when they were snatched up and torn apart. Still, the other dog and the cat were giving the deadheads fits. He sat down the lasso he'd unraveled from a nearby fencepost so he could let loose a third dog and a second chicken. Before him, the zombies had gathered back into two milling groups.

"Shit," Billy muttered from atop his fencepost. They didn't want them to do that. They wanted the zombies broken up individually. That way, Bobby would have an easier time snagging the one they'd chosen.

A white border collie, with terror in its eyes, darted between the legs of a male zombie missing an arm, and headed back toward its cage, tail tucked between its legs.

Bobby grunted something slick with salvia when he saw this one-armed zombie and the female they'd chosen shambling toward him, intent on catching and eating the beautiful collie. The nearby cat, hissing and spitting, was keeping the other zombies' attention.

The collie reached the gate and damn near leapt it, brown eyes pleading to Bobby for help. But the man ignored the trapped animal. He was all eyes for the zombie they'd dubbed Gary. He grabbed up the lasso and began twirling it over his head, hoping to lasso the zombie as it passed him by.

"Sddowfhwsss!" he screamed, as it dawned on him that the armless man would reach the dog first, well ahead of Gary.

"I'm on it," his cousin answered. Billy had been watching the chase. With one shot, he took the one-armed zombie's head clean off.

Bobby hooted with pleasure, and then kicked the fence with his boot. The collie yelped, then bolted back the way it had come. Gary, nearly atop the animal now, turned after the dog with a snarl. And that's when Bobby struck.

The rope swished out and fell silently from the sky to neatly envelope Gary, pinning her arms at her sides. He grunted and yanked hard, the rope growing taut. The zombie fell to her knees, and then spilled onto her stomach, hands and fingers twitching beneath the rope.

"GOSSSSRIFFF!" the man howled triumphantly.

"Fuckin' A, Bobby!" his cousin screamed from across the coral. As Billy slid down from the post, Bobby was tying the end of the rope to one of the cages. Next, he opened up the inner gate. Well away from him now, one large group of zombies was chasing the collie, which still eluded them, zigzagging crazily here and there. Eventually, the collie would leap the fence and escape the hellhole. The third dog released, a Beagle, was dead and decapitated. But the original cat still lived, as did the second chicken.

With the zombies scattered and far away, Bobby didn't have any trouble easing into the corral, pulling the girl into the space between the inner and outer gates, shutting and locking the first, opening up the second, and hauling his struggling prize to safety.

Gary snapped her teeth in Bobby's direction as he untied his end of the rope from the fence, threw it over his shoulder, and began pulling her toward an approaching—and grinning—Billy.

"Damn fine work, Bobby!" he said, slapping him on the shoulder.

"Okay, now pen her in the corner, just like I told you to." He was gesturing toward a horse stall that had at one time housed the Bower family's single horse, Run Like the Wind. Ever since that damned hunk of dog food had hoofed Billy between the legs, the stallion had forever been known as Run Like a Piece of Shit. This Billy kept to himself, since his daddy had loved the animal more than he'd loved Billy—often making that fact quite clear to his son. Sadly, Run Like a Piece of Shit had been partially eaten by two zombies during the first night the deadheads had broken up through the ground. What was left of the animal managed to escape the barn and attack Billy's father, getting hold of the man's upper torso and pinning him to the ground until the human zombies could catch up to them and finish him off.

The two hauled the zombie into the cool interior of their barn.

"Make sure those hands are secured, Bobby. I don't want her bustin' loose."

The zombie growled and thrashed. Once the bonds were tight, however, she began to whimper. She particularly feared the flaming torches gripped in their hands.

Billy looked at her with hungry eyes. Yep, the girl sure was a looker, all right. The best piece of female flesh the two had laid eyes on—well, in Bobby's case, a single eye—in quite a long time. She had a nice figure, with round hips and full breasts. And her face—by God!

Both men felt the sudden stir of arousal below.

She couldn't have been more than a couple of hours up from the spot where she'd laid down to die. And the wound the zombies had killed her with couldn't have been in a better location, as far as exterior beauty was concerned—a deep slash across the midsection, spoiling neither a pretty face above or dripping delight below. Okay, Okay . . . granted, some maggots had settled into the wound, festering there. There were also worms and adult flies buzzing in and out from the ripped-up abdomen. Not that the two really cared, mind you. They'd cornered worse than this Gary before them—women with no limbs, no legs or, once when both had been drunk stupid, no head. At least this one was nice to look at. She had most of her blonde hair intact, and wasn't missing a single facial feature. Not an eye, ear or mole.

"Yah! Yah! Yah!" Billy whooped as Bobby thrust the torch out toward the girl several times, causing her to stumble over the stall's raised doorstep—falling backwards into a specially rigged hammock. The ends pulled taut, and folds feet long and inches thick wrapped around the struggling woman's body, pinning her. Next, Billy threw aside his torch into a dented trashcan and grabbed hold the rope dangling down from the barn's rafters. With a grunt he put all of his weight against it, hoisting the zombie several feet into the air. Bobby moved in moments later, spinning her around until her backside faced the open stall. He motioned for his cousin to set her back down on the ground.

Now on her stomach in the dust, hay and dried manure, Bobby grabbed the woman's tarp-wrapped legs and spread them apart, turning away from the smell of rot that wafted up from the dusty spot there. He efficiently tied both legs to the wall. Billy was doing the same with Gary's arms.

"She secure?" he asked Bobby.

Bobby nodded, spitting saliva bubbles from the corner of his mouth.

Billy shrugged out of his coverall and moved up behind the naked female zombie. "Damn she's a looker," he muttered, and then had his way with her. Spent moments later, he stumbled back. Bobby came in next. He was blind to a thing called foreplay, which was probably a good thing. Had he approached Gary from the front, she likely would have reveled in tearing off his manhood. But from behind, the zombie was a helpless as a newborn.

Before long, Bobby began making an anguished growling sound. He finally broke away, and smashed his hand through the wall.

"What the fuck, Bobby?!"

Billy's cousin gestured toward Gary, mewling.

"What?"

Bobby again pointed to the trussed-up zombie's face.

He stepped over for a look—and frowned.

The zombie female was weeping. Both could see wet trails meandering down from those two, dead eyes, past the cheeks, and trailing into the snarling, blackened lips.

Billy kicked aside an empty bucket, while Bobby shattered more boards with a hammy fist.

"I can't stand it when they do that!" Billy screamed up into the rafters.

Neither liked the sound. It sounded too human.

Billy lit up a torch and used it to set Gary on fire. Bobby's second torch reduced the corpse into ash, which blew away in the draft blowing in from the barn's opened doorway.

Lighting up cigars afterwards, the two cousins wandered over to the door to cool off in the breeze. They looked out onto the fenced-in corral and the nine female and two male imprisoned zombies.

"Don't like the males," Billy said, blowing out a cloud of smoke. "We better kill them tomorrow, Bobby."

It couldn't be helped. The females, the two males and Gary, the one they'd just burned, had been members of a large migrating group just outside their property when the two had stumbled across them. Using chained dogs to lead them into the corral. But the males tended to dominate the females. So on the morning, Billy would use his Weatherby to drop the two males where they roamed. Then, with Bobby holding torches to keep the females at bay, Billy would set the two aflame.

Bobby slobbered something, and Billy nodded.

"Yeah, she was a good one tonight," gesturing toward the black heap on the barn floor. Two buckets of water had been dropped on the mess, lest the fire spread and burn the entire barn down to the ground. "One of the best we've had in a quite a while, in fact."

Today's catch had been the forty-fifth zombie subjected to the cousins' cruelty. The Dobson Brothers a mile to the south had a similar operation in place, and they'd reached the high 80s. But the Bower Cousins were always quick to point out their catches were usually to the point to where the flesh was liquefying, the smell alone making the "fuck-er" vomit over the "fuck-ee."

"You choose tomorrow," Billy said. "Okay?"

Bobby nodded. His one eye roamed the playing field. Finally he hooted.

"Which one?"

Bobby pointed.

"The one with blue jeans? That one? Well—" he started. "Jesus H! That one has no head! What the hell you turning us into, those Dobson dicks?"

Bobby groaned and hung his head.

"How 'bout the one in back? In the pink dress?"

Bobby nodded.

"Not bad. Pretty nice body. She has no arm, but that's cool." He nudged his cousin. "We don't care about arms, do we?"

"Ssfffhzz."

"You got it."

Bobby nodded more enthusiastically.

"Then we'll do her. Sounds good?" Billy clapped his cousin on the back.

His cousin nodded, then picked his nose.

"Well, I'm off for bed, then. You just make damn sure the door's locked and you shut off all the lights before getting into bed—even the closet light, 'ya hear me?"

Bobby nodded for a fourth time, his neck beginning to ache.

"Goodnight."

"Shjfout, nalfous," Bobby answered.

LOVE AGROUND

JESSICA McHUGH

PANIC IS A desperate man's greatest motivator. It turns the illogical into opportunity and long shots into last chances. At least, that's what Patrick Barnes believed as he marched through Lincoln Cemetery that night. But with each mossy tombstone he passed and the wind's whispered warnings, his confidence dwindled. He'd never walked the cemetery before, despite it being so close to his house he could say "Good morning" to Beatrix A. Harris from his kitchen window. In the thirty years he'd lived there, he never had, but as he passed her grave that night, he tipped his hat to her. Panic, though motivational, also held Patrick in a state of delirious fear. After seeing a strange ball of blue light scream from the sky to his backyard, who wouldn't be delirious or afraid?

However, in the boxing match between Patrick's fear and his curiosity, fear was TKOed within minutes. Patrick's brain started whirring from the moment he saw the light in the sky. He'd prayed for days on end for something, anything, to help him out of his bind, so when the heavens illuminated and cast a beam into the graveyard, he was certain his answer lay amongst the tombstones. In water as hot as Patrick was currently submerged, there was no reason not to try. He'd read enough "Amazing Stories" to know that sometimes the universe threw poor dogs like him a much-needed table scrap, and boy did he need one.

The blue light was either gone or too dim to see, but a line of broken treetops marked a path of destruction toward the mausoleums where, framed in char and scattered stone, a massive crater nearly swallowed him whole. He peered in fearfully, but there was nothing to fear; there was nothing at all. No aliens, no meteor, no light, no lump of airplane garbage. It appeared as if God had simply reached down and scooped out a lump of earth. He hopped into the pit, only then noticing the dead mouse. There was nothing special about it. It was as dead and dull as the rest of the graveyard. Then, he spied a shimmer of color behind its tail. He kicked the mouse aside to see a small, iridescent worm wriggling in the soil, and a blue glint in his periphery revealed more worms in the cavern walls.

The worms appeared normal except for the blue tinge at certain angles, but when the worm squirmed its way back to the rodent and buried itself in its open mouth, he realized it was anything but normal. As the last bit of blue disappeared behind its teeth, the mouse's tail waggled, its hind feet kicked, and it opened its eyes. Patrick jumped back in horror—and happiness. He could hardly believe it; not that the mouse had come back to life but that his prayers had been answered. Repeatedly panting "thank you, God", he yanked several worms from the soil and popped the sticky tickets to salvation into his 5-Hour Energy bottle. It filled up rather quickly and he was forced to empty out his water bottle and pop the rest inside. He ripped off his jacket, netted the furiously squeaking mouse, and ran home as fast as his weak legs would carry him. The miracle had come just in time. Farrah had been in the basement for two days and the whole house was starting to smell.

He'd been looking for an excuse to use the root cellar for years, but he never expected it to house something so horrifying, or precious. He opened the door with his eyes closed. He hated seeing her in that state. In life, she was so warm, so rosy. Now she was ashen, limp, and frowning. In the years he knew her, he'd never seen her frown. Death was bad enough, but sad was worse. The mouse shrieked as Patrick dropped it into a jar and dumped the worms onto the table. The few from the 5-Hour Energy bottle were dyed pink from the remnant liquid and curled themselves into squirming knots. He gathered the worms in his hands, and with a quaking sigh, he moved toward the root cellar. The stench plucked tears from his eyes, but he would have cried without the smell. He was so sad for Farrah. At least he wouldn't have to be sad for much longer. His prayers had been answered. He repeated it over and over. His prayers had been answered and his sins would be forgiven. There were doubts, of course, but he allowed them to be scraped away with each scratch of the reanimated mouse's claws against the glass.

"Everything is going to be all right, Farrah. You'll be back to your old self again soon. I'm certain of it."

He wasn't certain of it and he hated lying to her, but he hated her death more. She deserved to be as lively and beautiful as the first day he laid eyes on her, all those years ago when she served her first cup of coffee. Patrick was her first customer on her first day at Monroe's, but it was also a first for him; it was the first time he felt his heart really pound his chest, the first time he found himself absolutely speechless, the first time he deemed something "perfectly beautiful". But he could never muster the courage to tell her any of that. He simply admired her, and he wanted to admire her again.

He laid the worms on her arms and chest and they started squiggling like mad as they slithered towards her face. He didn't want to watch, but he couldn't look away. He was afraid the worms would hurt her somehow, and the last thing he wanted was for Farrah to suffer more than she already had. Some of the worms aimed for her parted lips while others opted for her ears. Only one pink-tinged worm was bold enough to enter through the stab wound in her throat. Once the last gleam of color vanished inside, Patrick listened for signs of life. He watched for her chest's rise and fall and held his hand above her lips with bated breath, but she never inhaled once. Despite the fact that she grabbed his arm, she never breathed.

"Where am I? What am I doing here?" she screamed as she sat up and looked around the root cellar. "Who are you?"

"Don't be afraid, Farrah. I'm not going to hurt you."

"Where am I? How do you know my name?"

Her fear was evident in every quiver. He wanted to hold her and assure her that things would be all right from then on, but every time he moved toward her, she scooted closer to the edge of the table. At least he could delight in the fact that her gray skin started to melt back to its original rose.

"Don't you remember me? From Monroe's?"

"Patrick Barnes? Two creamers, four sugars?" she asked.

"That's the one."

"Is this your house?"

"It's my root cellar, in my basement, in my house," he replied.

Her eyes grew wide and the quaking increased.

"It's okay. You're perfectly safe."

"What am I doing here? Did you drug me or something?"

"No! I'd never do something like that. I just—-I couldn't let it be true."

"What?"

"That you were dead."

Farrah sprung off the table and dashed out of the cellar. She grabbed a nearby shovel and brandished it as Patrick threw his hands up in submission.

"Farrah, please. I said I wouldn't hurt you."

"I can't trust what you say. You're obviously a crazy person," she spat as she backed up the stairs.

"I'm not crazy. Well, I am crazy about you, but other than that, I'm completely sane."

"Stay away from me or I'll bash your skull in, Patrick. I swear to God."

"You don't understand."

"Where's my cell phone?"

"Broken."

"By you?"

"No, by Harry."

"Harry who? Monroe?"

"Yes. He stepped on it, on purpose."

"Why would my boss step on my phone?" she asked.

"Because you were trying to call the police on him. Don't you remember any of this?"

"No. I don't know what you're talking about. Just stay away from me."

"Farrah, you can't leave like this."

"Like hell I can't. I'm going straight to the cops so they can throw your stalker ass in jail. You know, I really thought you were a nicer guy than this. A lonely guy, sure, but I never imagined you'd kidnap someone," she said.

"Then why do you think it now? I didn't kidnap you. Yes, it's my fault you died, but I didn't mean to hurt you. Please don't go. We can stay on opposite sides of the room. Just let me explain."

"Fine. Explain, but if you move one inch, I'm gone."

"I won't, I promise," Patrick said. "What's the last thing you remember?"

"Closing the restaurant. I remember locking up. Then . . . nothing," she replied.

"You don't remember Harry?"

"Harry didn't close last night. He had a party to go to," she started and crinkled her brow. "But I do have a feeling I saw him after that."

"He came back to the restaurant. He was drunk. He tried to kiss you. Does any of this ring a bell?"

"I don't know. It's all so fuzzy."

"What about the knife? Do you remember that?"

"What knife?"

"Touch your neck."

Her fingers moved up her throat and froze upon the wound.

"What is this?" she stammered. "A mirror. I need a mirror!"

"There's a bathroom at the bottom of the stairs. The door on the right. I won't move, I promise," he said.

She pointed the shovel at him as she descended the stairs and slipped into the bathroom. As soon as she flipped on the light, Patrick clamped his hands over his ears to muffle Farrah's scream.

"Oh my God, what is this? What did you do to me?"

"I didn't do anything. It's my fault, but I didn't do anything."

"I need a bandage," she screamed as she rifled through the drawers and emptied the medicine cabinet. "Do you have any Bactine? Oh my God, it looks infected. I look pale. Do you think I look pale?"

"Not as pale as you did."

"What's that supposed to mean?"

"Farrah, I'm not crazy and I'm not lying. You're dead. At least, you were dead."

"If I'm dead, why am I so lively?" she replied as she flailed her arms.

"Because I prayed for a miracle and I got what I wanted."

"You prayed for me to be alive? Why?"

"Because I care about you."

"You don't even know me."

"That's not true. I've watched you for the past three years at Monroe's. And unlike so many people I've seen walk in and out of your life, I've listened to every word you've said and remembered. I know how you wish you could eat cotton candy for every meal. I know how you wanted to be a concert pianist when you were little. I know how you think your red skinny jeans make you look fat. They don't, by the way."

"This is too much to handle right now. I have to get out of here. I have to get to the hospital."

"They won't be able to help you. If anything, they'll hurt you."

"What are you talking about?"

"I don't know how to convince you any better, Farrah. You're dead. Try to get your pulse if you don't believe me."

She slapped her fingers against her wrist with an indignant huff. After a few seconds, she pressed her fingers to her neck, then pressed her palm to her chest. She shook her head and looked up at Patrick with her hands trembling.

"What did you do to me?"

"Farrah, I told you—-"

"You said it was your fault. You said you didn't want to hurt me but it's your fault I'm dead!" she screeched.

"That's true."

"Stay away from me. I don't know what you did, but just stay away, Patrick."

She ran up the stairs and out the front door. Patrick sighed as he crumpled to the floor, wondering how long it would be before the police broke down his door. How long would it be before a doctor convinced Farrah she was dead and sent her somewhere for horrible, flesh-splitting tests? Imagining those scenarios was even worse than seeing her dead in his cellar. He couldn't let that happen to her. She'd just regained her light. She couldn't let the authorities take it from her.

The mouse squeaked madly as Patrick threw on his coat. He would have ignored it completely if not for the crimson paw prints he noticed on the glass. The mouse twitched terribly as its squeaks turned to screams. Patrick picked up the jar and looked at the bottom. He nearly dropped it when he saw the mouse's bloody stomach pressed against the glass. The iridescent worm was also pressed against the bottom, framed by seared skin and red fur. Its body burned a hole through the mouse and once the rodent stopped shaking, the worm wriggled itself out from under the limp carcass.

"Farrah," Patrick wheezed and flew up the stairs.

His car was gone. Farrah must have grabbed his keys. It was ingenious of her, but she'd always been quick-witted. She always knew the right wine to accompany any meal, and when a certain requested dish couldn't be made, she could always choose the best runner-up. It was one of the many qualities he loved about her.

Patrick hadn't ridden a bike since his thirties, but he didn't have any other choice. He freed the rusty ten-speed from the garage and threw himself into motion. His knees ached after only a mile, but he pushed harder. He aimed for the hospital, but when he saw his car parked in front of Monroe's, he veered toward the restaurant. As he squealed to a stop, he saw a shadow jerking in the window and feared he was already too late. The door was locked, so he peered inside and saw a shadow shaking again. But it wasn't Farrah's shadow. She stood still as Harry ran across the dining room and turned with a gun aimed at her.

"No! Get out of there, Farrah! Run!" Patrick screamed and when Farrah looked to the door, he saw that her stab wound was significantly larger.

It had been stretched across the front of her throat, but not one drop of blood stained her shirt. Harry spotted Patrick at the door and though there was murder in his eyes, there was equal horror.

"Farrah, let me in. Please," Patrick said and she nodded dazedly.

"Don't move, Farrah. Don't you dare touch that door," Harry warned.

She lunged for the lock and Harry fired. The bullet tore through her shoulder and knocked her back a pace, but she turned the lock and flung the door open.

"Harry, put down the gun," Patrick said as he stood in front of Farrah.

"You again? Jesus, what's your deal?" Harry groaned.

"My deal is trying to save this girl's life."

"I think we're a little past that point. I slit her throat over ten minutes ago and she's still walking around like nothing happened. She's not even favoring that gunshot wound."

"That's because you killed her a few nights ago."

"*You* killed me?" Farrah squealed at Harry.

"It was an accident."

"I watched you bury an entire blade in her neck. How was that an accident?" Patrick asked.

"I told you to leave and you wouldn't. You tested me and she paid the price."

"You really were trying to help me? I'm sorry, Patrick. I didn't know," Farrah said.

"You were in shock. Anyone would be."

"Oh God, what is going on here? Did you do some voodoo on her or something?"

"God answered my prayers. In my entire life, I never asked Him for anything. When I thought my heart would burst from loving you and never being loved back, I never asked him to dull my pain. Even when I got the worst news of my life, I never prayed for myself. But when I saw you fall that night, I knew I couldn't live without you. Even though you'd never be mine, I couldn't live without seeing your face, or making you smile, or accidentally brushing against your fingers when you handed me a coffee mug."

"That's pathetic. You're older than I am," Harry spat.

"I never had any delusions about our relationship. Unlike you, Mr. Monroe. You thought you could just take her."

"I remember now," Farrah said. "You came here drunk. You tried to kiss me. You tried to rape me, Harry. And Patrick saved me."

"No I didn't," Patrick replied sadly. "I tried, but he was too quick. He stabbed you and he left you to die."

"You're out of your gourd," Harry grumbled.

"Says the man who was too drunk to take the murder weapon with him," Patrick replied as he removed a tissue-covered knife from his coat.

"Is that my blood?" Farrah asked.

"Yes. The blood he spilled."

"She shouldn't have rejected me. And you shouldn't have interfered, buddy."

"And let you rape her?"

"She'd be alive instead of . . . whatever she is. A zombie, I guess."

"I'm not a zombie!" Farrah screamed. "Am I?"

"No, you're a gift from God."

Harry scoffed and aimed his gun at Farrah's head.

"Zombies don't come from God, buddy. I know that. And I know the only way to kill a zombie too."

"Harry, no!"

The gun discharged and Farrah hit the ground, but Patrick hit it hardest. He turned his back on the bullet and pushed Farrah to the floor before the shot knocked him on top of her. He rolled onto his back and howled in pain. Farrah eased him to his side and clamped her hand to the torrential wound.

"I am sorry about this, Farrah. Truly," Harry said.

"I trusted you. Why did you do this?"

"Like I said, it was an accident. None of this was supposed to happen, but now that it has, I can't just let it go. Move out of the way so I can put him out of his misery."

"No, kill me first."

"Why?"

"Because I'm fairly certain the extra time will give Patrick all he needs to kick your ass."

"That old guy?"

"He's only 52," she replied; Patrick couldn't help but smile at her accuracy. "And he looks damn good for his age. Better than you, thanks to all that booze."

"Now you're just being mean for mean's sake."

"How could anyone find you attractive? You're a monster, Harry. You hide it well, but in the moments between charm, it's easy to see the darkness in your soul. That's why I would never go out with you. You only *act* nice."

Harry's eyes widened and the gun shook in his fist. His breath became rapid, and with a vocal shudder, he flew out the front door.

"I don't know what happened, but he's gone, Patrick. Come on, I'll get you to the hospital," Farrah said.

"No, you can't go there. They'll know what you are. They'll cut you into pieces," he said as he looked up and choked back a sob at seeing her face.

A large hole had been burned through Farrah's forehead and a worm dangled from the mushy bone. The gash across her throat widened still as another worm squiggled from end to end and finally dropped to the floor.

"What the hell? What was that?" she squealed.

"It's my fault."

"Like my death was your fault? No, Patrick. You're my savior.

You're the gift from God," Farrah said as she wiped the blood from his face.

"There was a light in the sky. I don't know where it came from or what landed in the cemetery, but I found these weird worms. One wiggled into a dead mouse and brought it back to life, and I figured..."

"What are you saying? You put worms in me?"

A chunk of her forehead sloughed onto Patrick's chest and she screamed again.

"I'm sorry, Farrah. It looks like it was just a temporary fix. I wanted to save you so badly."

"What's happening to me?"

"I think you're dying, again."

"I don't feel like I'm dying," she said as a lump of cheek slipped from the bone. "Really, I feel fine. Great in fact."

"That makes one of us," Patrick sputtered.

"I'll drop you in front of the hospital. No one even has to know I exist."

"By the time I get stitched up, you might not exist. I can't say goodbye like this."

Patrick reached up and tucked her hair behind her ear. He tried to hide the fact that the ear fell off in his hand, but the worm that fell to the floor gave him away.

"Oh my God, I'm falling apart!" she wailed.

"I'm so sorry, Farrah. This whole thing is worse than if you'd just stayed dead. I made everything worse. But if it means anything, you're still the most beautiful girl on Earth."

"The most beautiful *zombie* on Earth," she whispered sadly, but a smile crept up her cheek and she giggled. "It's kinda funny, actually. Don't be sorry, Patrick. If you hadn't done what you did, I never would've known how you felt. Why didn't you tell me sooner?"

"Like Harry said, I'm an old man. You're a beautiful young woman."

"Not anymore," she replied.

"Your beauty was never physical alone," he said.

If her cheeks were intact, her blush would have been more apparent.

"Patrick, I'm not a child, and I'm not a bitch either."

"I know you're not. I'd never say that."

"Then why did you assume I would reject a wonderful man just because he's a little older than me? Do I seem that judgmental to you?"

"Not at all," he replied. "Do I really seem wonderful?"

"You seemed nice before, and I'm sure I would've figured out the wonderful part once I realized the sacrifices you would make for someone you cared about," she said, but when another worm dropped, she groaned. "I suppose none of this matters. Look at me. I'm done for, aren't I?"

Patrick didn't want to look her in the eye for fear of giving her hope or doom. He watched the worms curl and crawl across the floor instead. It was at that moment he realized the common trait in each fallen worm. They were the usual iridescent color, meaning each worm that burned through Farrah's flesh was one that hadn't soaked in 5 Hour Energy. There were still pink worms in her body, still keeping her animate.

"Where's the nearest store?" he asked.

"Store? Patrick, you need a doctor."

"I've seen enough doctors for a lifetime, believe me. You're the one who matters right now. Where's the closest store?"

"There's a convenience store down the street, but Patrick, you can hardly move and you're covered in blood."

"As long as I have a shirt and shoes, I'm sure they'll serve me," he chuckled. "Grab those worms and help me to the car."

He leaned against her as he hobbled to the car, but before she could open the door, he grunted and wilted to the ground.

"This is ridiculous! I'm taking you to the hospital."

"The store first, please. I need to get some 5 Hour Energy."

"I don't think an energy drink is going to help you, Patrick."

"But it may help you."

"Okay, we'll go to the store, but you're staying in the car. I'll wear a bag on my head if I have to.

She started rifling through Patrick's back seat. The pair of sunglasses sat askew thanks to her missing ear, and the kerchief she tied around the bottom half of her face made her look like a bandit, but when she showed Patrick her disguise, he smiled in adoration.

"How do I look?" she asked.

"Cute as hell."

"Is that a zombie joke?"

"A zombie compliment," he replied.

Even with the kerchief hiding it, he knew she smiled.

"What am I supposed to buy?"

"As much 5 Hour Energy as you can. For some reason, the worms that were in my water bottle rotted out, but the ones from the 5 Hour Energy bottle are still doing the job."

"But even if it works, if the worms keep me alive, or *undead*, the damage will still be done. I'll still look like this, like a monster. Won't I?"

"I guess so. I'm sorry, Farrah."

She removed the kerchief with a sigh. She caught a glimpse of herself in the mirror and with a whimper, started to put it back on, but Patrick stopped her.

"I don't see a monster."

"You're biased."

"I'm lucky," he said, even as his pain swelled and the blood loss made his head spin.

"Please let me take you to a hospital."

"There's no point, Farrah. It's over. I feel it as strongly as my love for you."

"This part is my fault," she whispered.

"No. I was doomed before this. I have stage four liver cancer. It was going to get me soon anyway. Don't be sad for me. Being able to finally tell you how I feel has been a wish come true. I just wish my love had been more of a blessing than a curse to you."

"Patrick, you have no idea how blessed I feel right now. Maybe this isn't how I imagined my life . . . or my death, but there's nothing to be done about it. Anyway, I'm lucky too. It can't be too often that a person learns how much they're loved after they've died. I felt loved by no one in life, but in death, I've learned that I was loved more than any other person in the world by the kindest man I've ever met. I wish I had known long before this, but knowing now is enough. I will take that knowledge with me and die happy. I don't remember how I felt the first time, but I know it was lonelier than this."

She squeezed his hand and kissed his cheek.

"On second thought, if the worms keep me alive, can I even die?" she asked.

"If you really want to leave this life, there's something we could try."

"I want to leave this life, Patrick. With you."

"I don't know much about the undead, but I know a shot to the brain always does the trick. I have a gun in the glove box. But there's somewhere I want to go first."

"Will you make it?"

"I'll make it for you," he replied.

When they reached the cemetery, Patrick was too woozy to walk. He could barely hold up his head, which Farrah used as an opportunity to drop one of her fallen worms on his shoulder. It squirmed into the gunshot wound and in a matter of seconds, Patrick's head lifted and his eyes popped open.

"What did you do?"

"Bought us some time," she replied as she grabbed the gun and helped him out of the car. "Where are we going?"

"Follow the broken trees, like I did."

"What happened here?"

"God. Something else. Whatever it was, it was a prayer answered. Just like you," he said and she stopped to gaze at him; he wanted to stay in that moment forever with Farrah looking at him like he'd always dreamed, but the sudden sear in his wound forced him to keep walking. "Quick, the worm is burning through. We don't have long."

They saw the barricade tape before seeing the pit. Not only had the hole been discovered, it had been excavated. The pit was larger and the sides dug deeper. He didn't know what had happened to the rest of the worms, but if they were collected, he feared how people with intentions far darker than his would utilize them. There wasn't a piece of him that regretted leaving the world behind.

They tumbled together into the hole, and though pain screamed through Patrick when he landed, he couldn't regret landing with Farrah in his arms. She pulled the pistol out of her pocket. The weight bent her wrist and she choked on sobs as she tried to lift it to her head.

"Wait, I have to say it again: I love you, Farrah. I've never loved anyone more. I don't care how crazy it sounds. I love you," Patrick whispered; her sloughing face would have been difficult for anyone else to caress, but Patrick reveled in any opportunity to touch her.

"I'm the crazy one. I didn't realize I loved you until tonight. Better late than never, I suppose," she hummed. "I just can't believe this has to end before it begins."

"Maybe it doesn't. Maybe this was the real blessing: right here, right now. This moment was my prayer answered. You believe in Heaven, don't you?"

"I don't think zombies go to Heaven."

"I don't think God believes in labels. And I don't think He judges us on one or two aspects of our composition. We do that ourselves. Besides, your current affliction touches no part of the real you: the woman I love more than life itself. Our new lives are waiting, Farrah. He'll let us be together, I know it."

Patrick grunted as the worm burned through his wound and popped out through his flesh. Farrah placed the gun in his hand and moved it to her face. The barrel against her temple made her shiver and moan, but when he thumbed back the hammer, her lips curled at him.

"Thank you for saving me, Patrick. And I don't just mean by bringing me back from the dead. Of all things we could be at the end of the world, alone would be the worst."

"Neither of us will ever be alone again."

"I believe you."

She grabbed the squiggling worm still half-embedded in his shoulder as he readjusted his grip on the pistol.

"One last thing," she whispered.

She pressed her lips against his and obliterated every nagging label stamped on them throughout their lives. They were ageless then, and as beautiful as ever.

Farrah tore the worm from Patrick's wound and he immediately felt cold death race toward his brain, but before the final freeze, he fired. The bullet charged through her skull and instantly stole the life from her eyes. She started to fall backwards, but he caught her and held her close before his own body keeled. Limp in each other's arms, Patrick and Farrah left the word "alone" behind with their empty shells in Lincoln Cemetery. They were discovered in the morning by two gravediggers who sought to take a quick whiskey break in the pit. What the workers thought of the man embracing a rotten corpse at the bottom, Patrick couldn't care. The beautiful young woman who stood beside him and flushed his cheek with the warmth of her lips made him laugh at their puzzlement, at the police's puzzlement, at the puzzlement of all who didn't yet understand the power of love in prayer. Patrick and Farrah's grave was not the freshest one in the cemetery that morning, but it was the deepest.

SONG FOR MAYA

KURT REICHENBAUGH

MAYA HUMMED THE the song into his chest. There must be less than three or four people in any given city on any given day that would know it, and Maya was one of them. A song by a band who'd disappeared somewhere before the end of the sixties, known since only to collectors of rare vinyl.

That she'd even know the song only intensified his desire for her, his need to be consumed.

He'd taken Maya to Bianco's, in Heritage Square in the Central district. Either a bad or good tactic depending on the company you were with. Getting a table at Bianco's meant waiting.

Maya resided in a cottage in the Coronado district downtown. His apprehension at leaving the comfort zone of his suburb in North Town only added to the allure of this girl he'd only known online.

Their conversations had been minimal, direct and carried by his side for the most part. They'd exchanged quick introductions, shared the bare basics of their equally dull occupations (his as an accountant and hers in some vague marketing research role) and other brief biographical details. On a whim he suggested dinner together at Bianco's and she agreed. Neither of them had been there before. He figured that if Maya turned out to be a stiff then nothing was lost in at least trying a new restaurant.

His pessimism came easily after his recent string of first dates.

There was Jennifer; a grad student in what she called "post-colonial studies" who lectured him endlessly about her travels to Delhi and Madagascar. He'd been to Canada, once.

Marcy carried on about how one should embrace old age. "Rock the gray," she said. Marcy despised anyone who dared assume she was young. "Like, hello people, I'm almost 30! Does that mean anything to you?"

Jeanine, the epidemiologist, frowned at his music selection. "Don't you have anything by Eritrean artists?"

Monica, a yoga instructor (how could you go wrong with that?) told him that she spoke Hungarian until she was six. "I learned it from our housekeeper who, like, barely could speak English. We used to have entire conversations right in front of my parents and all. They never had a clue what we were talking about, you know." He figured it wasn't the language barrier, but didn't say anything.

Rita, the poet, disapproved of his literary tastes. "Bukowski?" she sneered. "He's so derivative, and furthermore, a pig. I prefer Pablo Naruda, but in his native language. There's no other way to experience him, so much is lost in translation."

Then he met Serada. With Serada he hoped he'd finally found someone he could relate to. Like him, Serada had been an English major in school.

"Of course Mikhail Bulgakov wrote <u>The Master and Margarita</u>. I mean, duh!" Serada said.

He'd heard of neither.

"I always liked Zamyatin's <u>We</u> myself. Dystopian fiction torques me up like nothing else outside of Mickey Spillane novels." That was his attempt at a joke. One he hoped Serada would find amusing. She didn't. She ended the date early, letting him know several times how tired she was.

Weeks went by. He filled his days at the office churning through spreadsheets and financial reports, suffering audits from hell, wishing for something better in life.

Then, he found Maya.

I'm not going to give you the website he used. If it's something you're into you'll find it on your own. For now, it's their little secret.

He knew as soon as he read Maya's profile and saw her picture that he had to meet her. She was that distant green light seen from the back of a long line of traffic at rush hour. That vapor trail exploding against the sunset. That forgotten song that once burned fiercely above lonely hearts in the night.

He arrived for their date on time, maybe seconds early. Maya met him at the door with the deepest black eyes he'd seen this side of the solar system. She offered her hand, stone cool with black nails against his flesh. Music in the background, maybe Mazzy Star or something emo, vaguely familiar and dreamlike.

"So nice to finally meet you," Maya said. "I'm sure we'll have a wonderful evening."

Her voice. Some women have it and the rest would kill for it.

He wondered if Maya suffered the kind of hunger that he had. The hunger from loneliness in a world oblivious. She could smell it on him, he knew. Standing there in front of her, just another guy like any other she'd have passed going about her day, but for the mad longing of desire.

His car was clean and dry.

The stop lights were on their side.

"What's your favorite song?" Maya asked after they'd gotten their wine. At least, that's what he imagined she'd asked. Her words came slow, halting, as if spoken by someone who chose them carefully. They were sitting together on a bench outside Bianco's. The sun had gone down and the noise from 7th street had diminished.

He noticed her tongue against her white teeth, sharp, red.

"Don't tell me yours is something by an Eritrean artist," he said.

She shook her head. The tip of her tongue touched her upper lip.

"Thank God." He sipped his wine, taking a moment to think. "I'm not sure it's my favorite, but I can name one I bet you've never heard. Something that meant a lot to me once, when I was young."

Maya looked up at him, the candlelight between them reflecting in her luminous eyes.

"There was a Dylan song; 'Desolation Row'. I used to play it over and over, learning all the words. I would recite couplets from it to other kids at school. They thought I was weird. Already ten years gone by then; Disco dominated one camp, and people like Ted Nugent the other. Dylan was hopelessly outdated by then as far as the heads were concerned."

"Heads?"

"Burnouts, pot-heads, whatever," he answered. "You know, the kids in the concert jerseys who hung out in scruffy clumps in the smoking areas."

"Sing from it." Fingernails brushed his arm.

"I don't think I can remember any of it."

"Please." Her nails probed his flesh, cold.

He sang the first couplet, mentally hearing the dancing notes from the guitar accompanying him again. He felt seventeen all over, there with a mystery girl beside him and everything was life and death at once only no one else could see it.

"I like it," Maya said when he'd finished.

"It's kind of long," he paused. "What's yours?"

She shrugged, as though the question had confused her. He found the shrug captivating, the way her white shoulders moved.

Dinner lived up to the reputation Bianco's had. They shared their dishes, drank more wine, and left a big tip. It wasn't until after they'd departed the restaurant that he realized she'd eaten very little at dinner. He held Maya's hand (that cool stone wrapped in velvet) as they strolled through the square.

"Did I pass?" he asked.

She turned her head slowly, the dark eyes regarding him.

"The test, whatever standards you have that a guy must meet."

Maya smiled and nodded.

Coffee later at a joint off 7th Avenue that had once been an old gas station. They sipped their coffee among the disheveled hipsters who sat there perpetually wired and connected with their gleaming notebooks and phones. A guy with long hair and a beard sat at a makeshift stage, strumming a guitar and singing vaguely familiar B-sides. The guitar was almost quiet. They sat and listened, he glanced occasionally at Maya as she listened to the singer. Her eyes were lost in the dark. She'd pulled her long black hair into a loose knot so that it fell straight down her back. Her white shoulders begged to be caressed, long legs crossed, her skirt had risen above her knee. Toenails painted cerulean.

The set ended. The singer balanced his guitar on its stand and joined the girls working behind the counter, kissing the cute one with a Bride-of-Frankenstein hairstyle.

"Whenever you're ready to go home I can take you," he said "Just say the word."

"Already?"

Maya tossed him one of those Mona Lisa smiles. Some women can pull it off. Most can't.

"I know a place," Maya said.

It was an estate in one of the historic districts that had its own guest house. They stopped for a bottle of Malbec on the way. Maya pointed the way from the passenger seat in his car, sometimes speaking in a language he didn't know. The keys were waiting when they arrived, beneath a sun-bleached slat of a lawn chair.

They opened the wine and sat together on a small sofa near the bed. She'd found a pair of candles and matches in one of the cupboards and put the candles in two small jars. The moment had come and he kissed her.

After the kiss, he watched the most delicate, beautiful blue spider he'd ever seen, crawl from Maya's left ear. It crossed her shoulder, scuttled down her arm and into the cushions of the sofa.

The wind stirred the shadowy palms outside. A chime tolled.

She wore black satin, black satin on marble-white skin. He put his lips against hers and waited for the cool flesh to open.

Maya hummed the song then; the familiar tune by a forgotten band from the sixties out of somewhere in the Inland Empire. The one playing during his first dance so long ago with a girl named Veronica, who'd lied to him about not having a boyfriend. The one who first taught him that the best girls came with hearts of noir.

"I know that song," he said. "I know that song. It's by The Dovers."

Maya hummed wetly against his chest.

Later, in the bedroom, on his back. His hands and feet were tied firm to each bedpost with silk bindings. His left hand was wrapped in gauze, mummy-like. He could feel the phantom tightening of his fist against the binds. Maya straddled him, rising and falling. She'd let her hair down and he could see her small teeth as she moaned. Her long black hair draped over the both of them like a shroud. The insides of her thighs slick against his flesh and he moved with her, his limbs held fast by the silk. Forgetting all about the pain in his hand where she'd already removed three of his fingers.

He gazed up into Maya's face, her black eyes like fresh tar on an Arizona summer day, blue lips pulled back slightly revealing a red tongue running over needle-teeth, and he told her that he loved her.

He'd always loved her, ever since the first lie whispered into his ear by lips in the dark.

"Sing me that song, the one you told me about before," Maya said.

The words were almost lost between them, barely intelligible, spoken in a language he didn't know.

He began the first verse as Maya pulled the silk tighter and the spiders scuttled across his chest.

THE SHELTER

CHRISTOPHER LAW

THE STENCH THAT rose from the entrance shaft to the fallout shelter was almost overpowering. Without the medical mask, soaked in perfume, James knew he would be on his knees vomiting, as he had been yesterday. Today the waves of rot drifting into the New England sky competed in his nose with the nostalgic smell of his mother.

She'd been dead for almost a decade but her dressing table was in his parents room exactly as she had left it, one of two effective shrines in the once proud house a hundred yards or so across the unkempt lawn. Not all the perfume in the bottle had evaporated; he'd been relieved to find it.

Adjusting his bag on his shoulder, he swung himself onto the ladder and down, pulling the hatch closed. He didn't bother to lock it; he'd adjusted the wiring so the lights came on regardless. His father's clever security arrangements had been thoroughly compromised in the three years since his death, barely long enough for the furniture and books in his study to gather dust but long enough for the lawn to turn to shit, the shutters and external paintwork start peeling, a whole bunch of other crap James had never cared about.

The ladder was twenty feet, a metal guard protecting against a fall for most of the distance. The air at the bottom was clammy. When the task in hand was complete, James knew he'd need to run the ventilators solidly for a week, almost wished he'd chosen another location for the whole endeavour. If there had been more time to think he probably would have, but things had gotten a little panicked.

The problem didn't trouble him much; he'd never been one to spend long on regret and, truly, there wasn't anywhere else.

Stopping for a moment at the foot of the stairwell, looking at the closed metal door that led to the main body of the shelter, he readjusted the bag again. The contents were heavy, the sharp rim of a jar digging into the space between his shoulder-blades. The chore waiting for him behind the door was going to be worse than yesterday and regardless of how badly he wanted to see the end result he wished he could get there without having to go through it. He wanted a moment to prepare.

The entire edifice was, technically, illegal, but James' father had owned a construction company and been connected enough for the right eyes to close for a moment or two, now and then. Even after the man died, emphysema and grief eating his heart away before he hit sixty-five, James hadn't been able to discover what he had done before setting up the company. There wasn't a single hidden document, not even a suggestive note, to be found anywhere in the man's effects, nothing strange about the army pension he received. He was just another ex-soldier making good.

The interior door—the lobby door, his father had called it, every time he dragged his family below ground for a day or two of apocalypse survival training—had a submarine style lock James never bothered to seal.

It swung open easily when he pushed it with one hand. The hinges didn't creak since he spent an afternoon last week applying cans of oil, just to escape the sound. The stench grew worse for a moment as the pent up air washed out into the half-cleansed atmosphere of the entrance shaft; James stood still and breathed through his mouth, until the fumes of his mother's perfume started to irritate his throat, bringing on a coughing fit.

He tried to fight it but his chest wouldn't stop convulsing, his lungs choosing a poor moment to fight back against twelve years of smoking. He pulled the mask aside and hacked like an old man, sucking the decay deep inside his chest when he knew it was that or choke on the thin, sticky mucus coating his throat and sinuses. Eventually he drew enough oxygen to snort the snot into his throat, hocking thick phlegm at the wall.

It clung there, a solid chunk of virulent green stained with streaks of black, for a second before falling free. A stain was left behind but most of the mass fell quickly and landed with a splat.

Then the air tasted better and he could breathe freely.

"Acclimatised again," he said to himself, his vanity pissed no one could hear him sound so gravel-toned; his voice was normally far higher than he would have chosen. He stepped through the door with a smile on his face and looked at the scene before him, allowing the grin to broaden as he saw the changes twenty-four hours had wrought.

"Not much longer, babe. We're doing good."

The thing strapped to the bed thrashed and snarled, eyes permanently bulging because the eyelids had shrivelled away. The jaws worked mechanically but were too shattered to grab hold of anything, the mandible flopping on the throat every time the muscles relaxed. There were no teeth left in the rupturing gums, unless a few molars were still clinging on at the back. The nose was shrivelled and starting to collapse, the nostrils spreading up and out a little more each day. It was a shame that it was going to be lost, it had always been one of her best features, but there was nothing he could do to prevent the change.

"Feeling lively today?" he said, pushing the door shut with a foot as he stepped inside.

In his father's day the sizeable space had been occupied with utilitarian, almost comfortable tables and chairs, two waiting room style couches in one corner around a coffee table. There had been board games and a radio, a television and DVD player in later years. The walls had been painted cream with one given over to gun racks; dozens of weapons, from pea-shooters to assault rifles. Another wall had been given to cupboards of medical supplies and ammunition, all of them securely locked to prevent curious, childish hands getting hold. Leisure activities and maximum protection had both been important to James Senior's Armageddon Survival Plan.

The guns were still there, the racks left unlocked, and the ammo was kept in metal crates beneath them—still enough to supply a small army despite the hundreds of rounds James had fired in the forest since coming into his inheritance. The medicine cupboards were gone, the supplies that couldn't be used or sold for a high bundled into one of the two sleeping quarters branching from the main room.

Most of the old furniture had been pushed in there as well, until that room was full to the brim. Everything else had gone into the second sleeping area, except the television which was now a bullet ridden wreck in the undergrowth. The walls were still cream but they were hidden behind layers of thick velvet drapes, reds and blacks overlapping in an organic effect James loved but could never have created himself. More drapes covered the ceiling, billowing down in folds from the centre and the old, sensible linoleum floor was covered with thick, incredibly expensive scarlet rugs. The ceiling lights were hidden, replaced by tall lamps in the corners.

The four-post bed that dominated the space was something he could claim. Working all last spring and summer to his own design, he had carved every piece himself, carrying them down to be assembled. It hadn't come out perfect, there were joins in the base that didn't quite line up and he'd been forced to use wood glue in far too many places, but the flaws weren't visible to the casual observer. It was a grand, gothic beauty, embellished with gargoyles and patterns she had designed, stained and lacquered to look like ebony. The curtains were red velvet, currently tied back so he could always see the creature, and the sheets were all silk, white underneath and black on top. He didn't want to think about the hassle that getting the mattress in had been, if only because he knew he'd have to do it again if he ever truly planned to sleep down here.

The thing on the bed growled, the sound wet and choking, a thick gobbet of half-congealed blood running from one corner of the mangled mouth, adding to the thick deposits on the once pristine pillowcase. It arched its back, like a teenage girl in a possession movie and strained against the restraints, the distended stomach curving out like a pregnancy. He watched it for a moment, checking from a distance that the knots he had tied around the hands and wrists with the rest of the sheets still looked secure—the process wasn't far enough along to allow it any freedom.

A long, burbling fart escaped the thing's backside and he sniggered a little—the sound was straight out of the gross-out comedies he had always loved. The thing farted again, still straining to get free, and the pregnant belly deflated as the decomposition gasses escaped. Knowing what to expect he quickly put the perfumed mask back over his face and watched as a long, thick stream of pus and filth spurted out, adding to the thick cake of muck between and on the thighs, spreading out over the rumpled sheet and ruined mattress.

The latest stage of death expelled the thing collapsed back onto the bed and lay still, gasping and staring at him with blood filled, hungry eyes.

"Not much longer now," he said, crossing to the bed. He had brought a table and chair down, simply wooden things at odds with the rest of the room but essential in the short term, and he placed the bag on the table before sitting down. Looking the thing in the eye, smiling back at the malevolence, he started to unpack. "There's nothing too vile today."

Patti was already in her second year, majoring in medieval history, when James started at NYU. He'd spotted her a few days in, surrounded by books and glaring at the noisy freshman library induction tour he'd been on. Much later she had confessed to dismissing him as just another blow-hard high school brat, pierced and in black to piss off Mom and Dad, but for him it had been lust at first sight. He'd never tried to bullshit her and claim it was love; it had never occurred to him to be anything other than honest with her all the time, a first in his relations with girls. With anyone. The love had followed soon enough but it had started as lust.

For months after that first sighting he had tried everything he knew to score with her, both on and off campus. New York is a sprawl but they belonged to the same scene, one small enough to ensure they were often in the same place at the same time. Eventually she started to acknowledge his existence, their individual social networks inexorably interlocking, and eventually she'd stop to talk. Back in high school he would have taken steps to wear t-shirts for the same bands she did, mined their mutual friends to learn where she was going on the weekend, but he abandoned those ideas fast enough when he saw every other wannabe player get shot down, or used as a fuck-buddy for a few weeks, a month at most, before getting discarded—there was a small trail of broken-hearted freaks, boys and girls, in Patti's wake. It took until spring break to wear her down enough for things to really start, even then they hadn't been exclusive but everyone knew they had an understanding.

The following summer was a hard one for James. His father's health had started to decline and Patti disappeared to Europe. He'd spent the interminable time working in a video store and getting wasted, nailing any girl willing to spread her legs. There had been two pregnancy scares and one terrifying trip to the clinic—he came back clear, saved by a condom, but the girl at the source killed the man who gave her HIV before taking a swan dive off Brooklyn Bridge. James lost almost seventeen pounds, ribs visible when he took off his shirt and almost got himself disowned.

That was the same summer his little sister died; taken out when a drunk ploughed a stolen eighteen-wheeler into her school bus. She was three weeks shy of sixteen and died with eleven other children. The last two hours of the three hour chase went out live across the nation, James had been watching as it reached Echo Falls and the intersection a mile from the high school. As he sat in the shelter, staring into Patti's dead eyes, the moment his sister died had gotten almost a billion YouTube hits and there was a documentary.

Her room was the second shrine, eternally dedicated to some teen singer with abs and an allergy to shirts.

"You're not looking good," Patti said when they met at JFK, an extra three rings in her left ear and seven-pointed stars tattooed on her palms. "You look like you need a good meal."

That was the night they went exclusive. She broke him down and remade him. Just like the marines. Infatuation had turned to love and devotion. When she first asked it seemed natural to let her drink from his wrist, to accept the reciprocation when offered. It made sex even better.

The jar that had been digging into his back was the largest thing James took from his knapsack, putting it aside on the table. Originally it had been a two litre pickle-jar, a few letters from the word 'gherkins' still visible beneath the thick, black trails of encrusted blood running down the sides. It was full to the brim with a viscous mass of clotting blood and inner organs. Some of the blood was his and the rest came from the animals that had supplied the organs—cats were going missing across Echo Falls now that James had visited every pet store and rescue centre within an hour or two's drive a little too often.

Dogs were easier to trap and kill but have a better eye kept on them and, just for himself James preferred the promise of revenge he saw in a dying cat's eyes to the desperate acceptance in a dog's. There were a few squirrels in today's mix as well, plus the usual base of rats. His father's company was owned and operated elsewhere by other people but James had the keys to a derelict warehouse in the next town—a town large enough to have a slum area. Rats were plentiful there and, when it was time, one of the hobos he let break in would be useful.

Patti tensed but didn't struggle when she saw the jar, the black slit of her new pupils narrowing as she focused in on what she needed. It was the reaction he had been hoping for, the fourth day in a row. It was essential that she learn to accept his presence, to see him as the controlling force and not just lunch. If she didn't, and didn't soon, he knew he would have to end it, put a bullet in the remnants of her brain. The magnum he'd use if that moment came sat on the table, always loaded. When he was done with his other chores today he'd unload it, clean it the way his father had taught him, and load it again, leaving the safety catch off when he was done.

Established as Patti's consort James had chosen chemistry as his major, finally settling the battle that had raged between chemistry and physics since he was a kid. Disappointed in so many ways, Jimmy had always been proud that his son was a scientist, doing something useful. Patti guided him into the decision, still unwilling then to tell him everything, but he'd known it was the right choice from the start. He crowed with delight when he was finally told what her goal—their goal—was.

They had withdrawn from the scene, only venturing out for Halloween and a select group of bands, cutting out almost everyone they knew. Drug-dealers were the only ones they kept, uncaring about the resentment and derision of their former peers. They were onto something special, something that they alone could achieve. Patti dropped out and was disowned by her parents, taking a job in a sex-line call-centre instead. She gasped and moaned, said she was taller with Barbie tits, whatever was required, for double minimum wage until James Senior died, feeding them both and paying the rent from the couch, daytime soaps playing with closed-caption.

It was all pretty low-rent, but the haze of their plan and drug abuse had made it seem idyllic. Their apartment was roach free, an illegal sublet rent-controlled affair walking distance from a nice part of Central Park; a New York sitcom apartment. They stayed there even after his father died because they liked it, the exorbitant asking price given by the owner when they made the approach a snip to cover.

The accumulated profits from the sale of the company and the insurance payouts had left James stinking, filthy rich. Twenty million alone came from the death of his mother, one of forty-three people flown into a mountain by a drunk pilot—the airline was bust and a lot of people were in jail for negligence, even, rarely, the CEO. Another million came from his sister's death; the state paying out handsomely. All that plus his father's insurance gave him enough for a Park Avenue pad, if he'd ever wanted one.

"I know you don't like this, babe," he said, rising from the chair and leaning above her abdomen, confident her attention was fixated on the jar. "But I gotta do it."

There was virtually nothing of her stomach left; it had been torn out by the branch she landed on. The entrails, or as much as he could find, that had fallen free had formed part of her first meal – nothing else to hand and the first meal needed fast. He'd left the mangled form of the girl below the branch, her current boyfriend over the boot of the burnt out fifty-seven Chevy. The sixteen year olds had been planned for something else, but he'd been forced to adapt, frame them for the crash.

Poking at the healing flaps of skin—her belly would end up concave—he looked for signs of infestation. It was summer and flies were thick in the air outside; no matter how he tried he couldn't prevent a few sneaking in when he opened the hatch. That was why her nose was gone—he hadn't noticed the maggots until they started to drip from her left nostril one day last week. Her nose had survived the crash, his negligence had ruined it. He found nothing but the semi-liquid mass of her insides draining away, the desiccated remains keeping her alive, working with the potion he had found in Patti's recipe book.

"Almost there," he said, straightening up and watching the goop drip from his fingers. The black nail varnish was chipped and he had major hangnails. "Not much longer now."

The recipe book was something Patti found in Europe, printed from digital images of a secret book in a hidden library; a text and place every true black witch and Crowley devotee knew from legend and rumour. In their apartment, secluded and just high enough to be lofty, they cracked the code and with all he learned James concentrated the recipes, reducing them to their chemical core. They bought almost one-hundred gerbils and killed them making sure they were right, flattening the last proof they needed under their car because it just wouldn't die and kept biting.

In the last few months they had reached the stage the book proscribed, injecting themselves daily with the essences James created in his lab—a thirteenth floor Bronx apartment. They kept the track marks hidden beneath long-sleeved shirts, added others with heroin. They had readied themselves, changed their very existence at the atomic level with the concentrated knowledge of European cunning women; they had been ready for the next stage.

Luring the teenagers out had been easy. Free drugs and booze; a ride in a truly cool, chrome-laden beast—a red '57 Chevy called, of course, Christine. The promise of a visit to The Shelter had only sealed the deal—who'd want to miss an all night party in a fallout shelter? The only thing they fell faster for was the sedative in the whiskey. Patti had taken footage as James stripped the two naked and hog-tied them, leaving the camera filming as they fucked in front of the waking youths. Afterwards he had used a marker pen to outline their jugular veins, the points he intended to tear open and drink from. They'd left them there, alive, for a few hours to go on a beer run.

It had all been planned out, had all been so easy to achieve. Nothing seemed like it could go wrong.

Returning from the liquor store he'd pushed Christine close to a hundred, playing chicken with nocturnal blind bends and the surrounding trees. Patti hadn't been wearing her seatbelt, she never did. They were only a quarter mile from home when a tire blew on the final bend. The car span round and flew over the crest of the short verge and into the trees. In slow motion he saw her sail through the window, glass falling all around, through the air and onto the broken branch, itself the victim of an earlier crash.

She screamed the entire time it took to get her down, as he clambered on the crumpled hood, slipping in the blood and foetid innards spilling everywhere. Somehow she had stayed alive for most of the distance to The Shelter, coughing blood onto his chest as he ran through the trees, adrenalin giving him strength. After she died he kept running, knowing it was too late for the original spell, the one the teens had been taken for, but desperately concocting Plan B. Back underground, the teens screaming through their gags, he had prepared the concoction, fed Patti with her own guts and his blood. Saved his true love's life. Sort of.

Killing the teens had been easy, a simple cyanide injection. He'd wanted to keep their corpses, as food for Patti, but the crash required a cover-up. Using his father's car, gasping with relief when the battery wasn't dead, he'd ferried the dead teens back to the Chevy and spent almost an hour arranging them as best he could to match the scene. He salvaged the girl's stomach and intestines, after heaving her onto the branch. An hour later, as dawn was breaking and after a long shower, he reported Christine stolen. The police never looked that hard, treating the situation as an obvious open and shut case. The funerals had been a few days ago, James had sent flowers.

"We're almost there," he said to his girlfriend as he straightened up from inspecting her, satisfied that the change was almost complete and going well. She'd never be beautiful again, and her eyes would always be savage and hungry, but she'd be back with him, as loyal as any Haitian zombie could ever be. Just a few more days, a few more doses of the mixture that would keep her from attacking him. He was sure.

"You hungry, babe?"

She looked at him for a second; flickers of intelligence in her swollen eyes, glaring at the jar of bloody mush. The question was stupid, would always be stupid—zombies are always hungry—but he felt better asking it. Patti was never going to speak to him again, but he was never going to stop talking to her, albeit the way some people talk to their pets. In time, he was sure, he'd learn how to read her responses; he'd done it with his mother's cats.

Lighting a cigarette he sat down again and unscrewed the jar, pulling free a strip of rat gut that he dropped into her mouth, like a hungry baby bird. She snapped it down, the broken jaws managing to close long enough for her to inhale it. A few seconds of gagging and convulsions followed as she fought the lump down her throat. He watched her larynx bulge against the skin of her throat, distending the barbed wire choker she'd had tattooed. When she was done he fed her the second strip, dangling it carefully so it slid down her throat as straight as possible.

As a child he'd grossed out his sister by swallowing strands of spaghetti the same way and them pulling them out intact.

"Thatta girl!" he cooed as she took the third piece neatly, hypnotised by the movements of his hand.

There were almost two dozen concoctions in the book Patti found, split into three rough sections—mischief, malediction and metamorphosis. Mischief was the largest and they had used it to perfect their skills. Spiking people's drink so that they woke up with warts or hairy palms was as delightfully fun as the time he cherry-bombed a toilet in eight grade—twenty in the pan and a week at home. They'd only used two from the middle tier; inducing a miscarriage in a waitress they saw spitting on someone's food and an aneurysm in a high-profile rapist who escaped on money and a constitutional technicality. His brain ruptured on the steps of the courthouse, slimily defending himself, at the exact second they finished the incantation. There was no question as to cause and effect.

Delicately dropping the last shreds from the jar into her mouth, James put out his fourth cigarette—feeding her took an hour. She kept glaring at him, her eyes seething and alive, demanding more, looking at the jar. It held a broth of blood and sinew, small chunks of raw meat, filling almost a third. He wanted to give it to her, the bonds were still secure, felt the twinge a weaning mother must feel. Eventually she'd get it, but there were dangers in overfeeding. The secret text made that explicit. She had to digest for an hour or two before drinking.

There were only two recipes in the metamorphosis section of the text, although they formed half the total work. Little potions are as easy as any other recipe, fundamental changes to existence a little more complicated.

"Wanna be a vampire?" Patti had asked the day she shared everything with him. "Could be fun, huh?"

The dead teens—their joint history of grand theft auto helping the police not to look too closely at anything—had been taken as a first meal. The girl for James, the boy for Patti. After the dead, crumpled youths lay on the floor they had planned to suck deeply from each others throats, inflicting hickeys with fangs.

The Shelter should have been a boudoir, a vampire's den. Instead it stank of rot and there was slime accumulating on the velvet. All their dreams were broken and shat on; he was just trying to make the best of a bad situation. He'd screamed at the moon the night after she died, howling until he lost his voice. It would finally be full tonight and amongst the other things in his bag he had a bottle of whiskey, just waiting to be drunk. Just something to help him let it out.

Another two weeks passed the same way. The daily routine of trapping and killing small animals, draining blood from his own arm, grew almost monotonous and he had to venture farther into the woods every morning to find enough. It would have been disheartening if the progress hadn't been so clearly visible; her behaviour increasingly docile and the wounds steadily sealing over. Her appetite didn't diminish by a speck but gradually he was able to lower the other ingredients, the distilled herbs that would make her more than the slavering monster she had been at the start.

Eventually, however, he was confident that the process was finished—thirty days after the crash.

Her toothless jaw still hung open most of the time but the muscles and bones had fused adequately enough to allow her to chew without everything falling free. The skin over her eviscerated abdomen was thick, knotted scar tissue, white at first but quickly blending into the greenish grey of the rest. After a large meal the concavity grew swollen enough to almost flatten out, revealing the fact that her navel had survived the impaling. He found one of her rings in her bedroom on the twenty-ninth day and carefully re-pierced it for her – she'd always loved her belly-piercing.

There was nothing he could do for her face, the nasal cavity an open hole that would never close and her eyes forever bloodshot, but, as he finally released her from her bonds, he thought she looked as beautiful as ever.

"You wanna eat me, babe? Now's your chance."

She looked at him as she rose, gurgling in her throat and for a second he thought he would have to use the magnum after all. Then she just stood there, eyes fixed to his face for a small eternity before, finally, pointing at the jar of rat guts he carried, asking to be fed.

"Anything you want," he said. "You got it."

He kept Patti for almost a decade before she escaped, never getting around to completing the original plan. It wasn't a surprise when he came home to find the hatch open and his lover gone, he knew he'd been getting lax in recent months but couldn't bring himself to care. The daily grind of keeping her fed had worn him out years ago—the woods around his home had been silent for a long time and the Feds knew there was a killer in the area. Even the kisses and half gentle caresses weren't enough to make him care anymore. They had as much meaning as the hours he spent playing video games, drunk and high, never short of a fresh supply.

It was almost a relief for James when he entered the woods and she pounced from the undergrowth, sinking incredibly strong fingers into his throat to tear free the flesh her toothless gums couldn't tackle. She sucked on the wound for a minute or two but rose while he was still alive.

"Always together, huh, babe?" he gargled through his wound as she sat down to wait for the change to take him. "Love you too . . . "

WAITING IT OUT

ROB MOSCA

ZEE FLICKERS INTO consciousness from a deep black out sleep, a candle flame of awareness sputtering back to light. She's buried alive under an avalanche of blankets and coats unconsciously spun around her into a cocoon.

Her face emerges from an opening in the covers, wincing at the harsh gray light that floods the eyes. Slowly Dave's outline is sifted from the glare, a fuzzy shadow framed within the room's sole window. She vaguely registers that he is standing there with his back to her, before a cold draft splashes her face and sneak snakes through the modest opening within the blankets to send a shiver down the skin.

"Come back to bed, baby," she mutters, rolling the cocoon to its side and planting her face deep within a crumbled wall of pillows lining the bed.

"I can't sleep," an unfamiliar voice answers from somewhere within the room.

Zee struggles free of the covers and bolts upright in the bed.

"Dave!" she shouts out to the apartment beyond the room, struggling frantically for release from the sheets that have suddenly straight jacketed themselves around her.

"Paul," the shadow corrects with an exhausted sigh, one that comes from having done so far too many times now. Paul turns from the window and unveils a half hearted smile that delivers in its passing a soothing recognition across Zee's frozen gasp. It only takes her a moment to remember that Dave is long gone and that she lives (if you can call it that) with Paul now. It takes another to realize that he's standing there naked—bringing with it an acute awareness that under the blankets so was she.

'*Well at least we finally got that out of the way . . .* ' she thinks, shrugging her arms free from the bindings of the bed and rummaging through the night stand ashtray for a cigarette butt, '*. . . shame I can't remember whether or not he was any good .*'

"What time is it?" she asks, not knowing what else to say.

"Why?" Paul snorts a humorless laugh, "You got somewhere to be?"

"Suppose not." She lights the butt like it was a roach and savors the drag. Paul turns back to the window, his arm propped against the frame and resting his head against it to take in the view.

"Aren't you afraid they'll see you?" Zee asks, stretching into a yawn that sends the cold hardened nipples of her generously weighted breasts to peek out before sinking back beneath the blankets.

"Nah, not really. Not anymore . . . " Paul shrugs completely missing the show, "they don't seem to look up for some reason. Guess, that much about them hasn't changed."

Charged silence, neither knows how to broach the subject of what happened between them the night before. Zee lights a second butt off the cherry of the first and asks without interest—

"How many out there today?"

"Shit, I dunno . . . more than a hundred, two maybe."

"More than yesterday."

"Definitely."

"What do they want?"

Paul looks slightly over his shoulders towards her. Half his face lit up, revealing the beginnings of a stubble beard that does little to hide his gaunt cheeks.

"You *know* what they want."

"But how do they even know we're here?" Zee protests, her frustration amplified by the absence of more cigarette butts to draw upon.

"Dunno . . . instinct maybe?" Paul shrugs and turns his attentions back to the window.

A sudden crash goes off in the apartment below.

Zee's eyes go wide with a terrible apprehension. She pries her stare off the hardwood floor and up unto Paul, who remains stone still before the window as if nothing had happened. Covering her mouth in fear, afraid the faintest breath will betray her location, she listens carefully. The power and the heat having been cut off long ago, there is no ambient noise to filter out the intrusion.

Cascade of smashed dishes, followed by an excruciating crunch of footsteps on broken porcelain. The sound of it, for some reason, reminding Zee of walking across a field of virgin snow one distant childhood winter ago. An elongated yawn stumbles into a croaking moan. Crackle of smashed wood, slap of toppled bookcase.

"They're here," Zee whispers, hoping she's wrong, hoping she's not hearing what she's hearing.

Paul nods slowly at first in response, then continuously as if in a trance, refusing to look away from the window to address her. He sniffs violently and it is at that moment Zee realizes that he's crying.

***

ELEVEN DAYS AGO, which was only two after the Shit Storm of the Century first hit and the American Apocalypse went from bad to biblical overnight.

There was still power then and Zee sat on the edge of her bed cross-legged, watching the news on mute and chain smoking her way through a carton of Winstons. The ticker at the bottom of the screen scrolled the same continuous instructions and CDC updates in stark contrast to the nightmare imagery that flashed frantic before her. Zee took it all in with stoic detachment. At her core was a stubborn refusal to accept the stark reality being broadcasted into her skull non-stop. It was too preposterous to entertain seriously.

Not that the world was ending, but rather how. Floods, famines, nuclear war, hell even that old classic . . . the giant meteor plummeting to Earth, that, that she could live with. Even if this had been an ordinary epidemic, she could accept that a little easier. Sure it would suck and she would still be frightened, but at least that made sense. An outbreak of some sort of 'super-smart virus', though? One that supposedly wasn't finished with you even after you were dead? No, it was just too stupid to be taken seriously. A hackneyed plot to any number of bad movies at best.

But still, it had been hours now since Dave left for the store to stock up on supplies and he hadn't returned yet. She buried that thought deep beneath the television glare that she basked in, though it continued to claw away at the bottom of her attention.

A light tapping at the window startled Zee out of her reverie. She scrambled off the bed, forgetting she was sitting cross legged, falling comically behind the mattress and popping back up with hands trembling together the barrel of a .38 special.

It was night time and she could only make out that the outline through the window. It was crouching outside on the fire escape before the pistol sent it to jump back in panic.

"Please, y'gotta let me in." A male voice, high pitched with panic and cracking at the vowels, "Those things are all over the place."

"I have a gun!" Zee shouted back, instantly realizing how stupid that actually sounded in real life as opposed to on TV. Obviously she had a gun. It was right there between them.

"Lady . . . " the man began, before Zee cut him off.

"My boyfriend's here and he's got a gun too."

"Yeah, well he'll need it . . . " the man laughs nervously and crouches back down after casting a cautionary glance over his shoulder. Paul's face presses against the glass, clean shaven, fleshed out, twenty years younger than the stranger's reflection he'll see two weeks later looking back at him. "Look, lady, please, if they see me up here they might try to follow . . . "

"I don't care." Zee stands up, the shaking hands steady with a breath into a dead shot centered on Paul's brow. When Dave bought the .38 home, shortly after they had moved to the city, despite her protests to the contrary he insisted she learn how to shoot it. In time Zee came to enjoy their weekend visits to the range, developing quickly a proficiency with the weapon, and though not a marksman, became quite an accomplished shot in the passing of scant months.

Paul stares up the barrel to the narrowed green eyes behind the pistol, behind the window and finds no bluff waiting there. Suckling his lower lip in dire contemplation, something catches his ear below him. Glancing down, his face drains into slack jawed terror, before slicing back to look up at Zee.

"Sorry, but I do," Paul answers with a press of his palms against

the flat of the pane. With a gentle but insistent force he begins to test the window. It budges slightly. Zee didn't, despite having scolded Dave countless times for doing so, forgot to lock the window.

Zee clicks the hammer back. "Go somewhere else, then."

"Yeah . . . like where?" The window rises only slightly, but it's enough for him to slide his fingers under the frame.

Zee steps forward, driving the potential of the shot closer. "Anywhere. Just not here."

Paul snorts in frustration staining the pane with a splotch of fog. His fingers wait impatiently under the frame. His face floats in the belly of Zee's reflection against the glass.

"I don't think y'understand, lady. There ain't no 'anywhere' left." His words flow hush hissed with stressed urgency. "Those, those . . . whatever the fuck they are . . . had me cornered down there. I had no way out but up. Now I don't think they saw me . . . but the longer we stand here talkin' the sooner they're gonna figure something out ."

Zee doesn't answer. It is more than his words alone she is hearing. Even with the window only slightly open, the absurd, bad news on the television (that she had previously banished beyond the walls of her denial) now floods the small bedroom with a relentless torrent. Siren flocks wail incessantly, failing to drift off into the anticipated Doppler echo. Incomprehensible commands squawk through a distant bullhorn before being truncated in a sudden crackle of gunfire. The room shakes with the passing sweep of a low flying helicopter. The framed picture of vacationing Dave and Zee, rattle walks to the edge of the nightstand before making a suicide leap off the ledge to fall face down on the floor. Someone starts screaming from down the street, until they're lost under the rising tide of a vast collective groan.

"Look, here's the deal." Paul wills a diplomatic cool into his voice, one reserved for the coaxing of small children away from a potentially bad habit. "You got a gun. I don't. I'm coming in anyway, 'cause right now I'll take a bullet over taking my chances back down there. So you do whatever it is y'gotta do."

The pistol has become too heavy to hold against the cacophony of the outside world and Zee lowers the barrel to the floor. Paul yanks the window up as far as it will go, before clambering and crawling head first into her life.

***

ZEE SITS LEANING into the opening of Paul's hug on the edge of the bed. They sit there watching the dresser, the TV stand, the night table and small bookcase all clumsily piled into a barricade across the bedroom door.

It's been two hours since they first heard the commotion downstairs and things have only gotten louder since. They've managed to get to the front door of the apartment, their march heralded by the creaking of the steps under the weight of their somnambulant march. They started banging on the door almost immediately after the hall corridor filled up. Slow and without rhythm, a horde of drunks who have all lost their keys in the middle of the night, trying to rouse their loved ones from the grave of sleep to let them back in. This close and now the couple can hear that each moan, each groan, each death rattle sigh and gurgle possesses a distinct voice.

"Don't s'pose we got any of that Vodka left." Paul snorts a weak laugh.

"N'uh." Zee shakes her head slowly as if emerging from a distant dream, "We finished it off last night, remember."

"Whadda we got then?"

"Just the last of the tap water and a couple spoonfuls of instant coffee for flavor.

"Pass . . ."

"Yeah, same here."

They sit there for another minute before a sharp, splinter crack snaps them into a mutual jolt. The front door of the Zee's apartment has been clearly breached with the groans decidedly louder now through the opening.

"Hope you remembered to put the chain on." Paul forces the joke through the throat choke.

Zee doesn't say anything. She looks down at the .38 nested in her bare lap. She looks back up at Paul. "Hey."

"Yeah."

"How do you, you know, want to work this out?" she says, her eyes dashing between his face and the pistol to connect her meaning.

"I, uh, I dunno, hadn't really thought that part out yet. I mean, I can, um, take care of you first." He stammers before an embarrassed realization dawns upon him, "I mean, that is if you want me to."

"No, that's okay . . . I'll take care of me. I just meant do you want me to go first, or do you want me to, well . . . help you out before I go."

The last remnants of the apartment door explode. The slap dash barricade of book shelves topple over, the couch bolstering them slides with a scrape against the wall, sound of bodies falling over one another in a somnambulant stampede. Shuffling footsteps and starving animal growls approach the waiting couple.

"Jesus . . . what a fucked up way to go." Paul shakes his head with anger. "You remember how on TV, back when all this shit started going down, how all those religious types started telling everyone that this was God's punishment. For the gay marriages and Obama and all that shit. Well, y'know what? If this, if all this, is God's doing ... well fuck him! I'm not giving the bastard the satisfaction. You do it, okay. I want it to be you, not Him, not them. You, you pull the trigger when the time is righ t... and don't you dare fuckin' miss!"

"We could try the fire escape," Zee suggests, laying a reassuring hand on Paul's lap. "It got you this far."

"Have you seen it down there?" Paul snorts dismissively.

"We could make a stand . . . " Zee holds up the pistol and levels it at the bedroom door.

"I . . . I can't let *them* be the last thing I see. I'm sorry."

"No, it's okay. I understand. I'll . . . I'll take care of you." She lowers the pistol and looks up to Paul. He's begun crying again. Softer this time than before. He leans into her body and she drapes a hug around his shoulders. It's not long before they drift towards a kiss as the bedroom door starts buckling under a chorus of pounding fists and croaking groans.

Paul pushes forward, flattening her down across the bed beneath his weight.

She shifts her thighs out from under him and wrap them around his waist. With a fumble and a little help from her hands, he slides and buries a warm death into her. A small bird call escapes the cage of her throat with a gasp.

A grasping hand bursts through the thin plywood board, a stench of rotting meat permeates the room.

Paul's thrusts speed up, Zee's groan is raised in defiance to the waves of hungry growls around them.

Wave fire courses beneath dark skin layered in a coat of goose bumps, as Paul's slackens into thankful oblivion. Zee barks a satisfied curse towards the sky, meeting the splashes of hot death between noose tightened thighs and a raising of the pistol to Paul's temple.

MAXWELL'S SILVER HAMMER

ROB SMALES

"DAMN WATER DAMAGE! I can't make this out—Ben, can you decipher this?"

Dr. Maxwell thrust the travel-stained note across the desk at him. Dr. Benjamin Binder took it, glancing at the weatherbeaten package on the desk, its brown paper wrapping torn at the top like a Christmas present given to an excited child. He focused on the note in his hand.

"Let's see . . . you're right, this really *is* a mess . . . "

Maxwell made an impatient gesture. "Yes, but can you read any of it?"

Ben held the paper up to the light.

"Well, there's a whole section right in the middle that's nothing but a blur—wait, there are a few words here. 'Powerful'. And this says 'never seen before'. Toward the end it's talking about 'controlling the heart', and 'absolutely amazing', and then just this last line, 'beyond our wildest dreams'."

He held the limp note out to his mentor, who took it with a trembling hand.

"That's about what I could get out of it too," said Dr. Maxwell, gazing into the open package. "But do I dare use it, without knowing the whole story?"

That last was a murmur, more to himself than to Ben.

"Sir," said Ben, resisting the urge to just lean over and look in the open box, "if you don't mind my asking, what's all this about?"

The old physician looked at Ben with an expression of surprise, then nodded.

"That's right, you don't know anything about this, do you? Of course, we weren't supposed to tell anyone anyway. Let's see . . . do you know Bill Harrison?"

"Dr. Harrison? Yes, I met him when I started here, but he went on sabbatical shortly after I arrived. I've never actually worked with him. Rumor is he's looking into retirement, using his sabbatical to see what it's like not to work for a while."

Dr. Maxwell waggled a hand.

"Yes and no. People came to that conclusion on their own, and I haven't dissuaded them, but it's really the opposite of that."

Ben's eyebrows climbed skyward.

"Beg pardon?"

Dr. Maxwell paused, smoothing a hand over his shock of white hair. His cheeks darkened, and Ben realized the old sawbones was actually embarrassed.

"Look, Ben, . . . I know what everyone thinks of me. I'm the oldest doc on staff, and Bill's right behind me. We were in med school together, and that was back before you were born. We know everyone's just waiting for us to retire—looking forward to it, even. The thing is," he took a deep breath, then sighed, "we don't want to."

Ben felt awkward about this conversation. Maxwell was right, the entire staff was anticipating his retirement, but Ben didn't think it politic to confirm that right now. He settled for nodding, and saying, "I see."

"We both love the work. That's why neither of us ever went into Administration—we want to stay in the field. But medicine is changing fast. Years ago, we were the hotshot young docs on the floor, but now we're falling behind the times. There's still a lot of good we can do, but not while people are treating us like a couple of broken-down horses, ready for the glue factory. We were discussing this when Bill came up with the plan."

Ben pointed to the package on the blotter.

"This is part of the plan?"

"I'll get to that in a minute. Bill's idea was to try to get our edge back. New techniques come out every day, there's no way we could keep up. He wanted to go old school."

"Old school?"

"He went on sabbatical so he could travel to places where they look at medicine differently. He was hoping to find something so old it had been discounted by modern medicine, but so effective that it would look like a miracle to you young docs."

Ben pointed again.

"And that would be this?"

"It's got to be! I've gotten letters, occasional phone calls, but now he's actually *sent* something!"

Maxwell reached into the box and withdrew a jar holding about a pint of pearlescent gray liquid. As the light glinted off the glass the fluid roiled in response to Maxwell's motion. Ben thought it looked somehow organic.

"What is it?"

Maxwell shook his head, his attention fixed on the jar.

"I have no idea. It's from Haiti, according to the postal markings, but it got soaked somewhere along the way. That note we can't read is the only explanation Bill sent, but it *has* to be something special! According to the note it seems to have something to do with the heart, but I just don't know . . . "

He put the jar back into its nest, then swept the box from Haiti into a lower desk drawer, saying "Well Ben, it's time. Are you ready for tonight's festivities?"

Ben smiled. Though he *had* been anticipating Dr. Maxwell's resignation sometime soon, he still admired the man's love of the job.

I hope I still look at a night working in the ER as 'festivities' when I'm his age, he thought.

But all he said was "Yes, sir," as the two of them walked out of Maxwell's office, toward the Emergency Room.

***

"THE MEDIC ALERT bracelet says she has a congenital heart defect," shouted the EMT working the bag valve mask.

"How long has he been working on her?" Ben gestured to the man riding the gurney side-rail as it rolled, counting aloud as he continued chest compressions.

"Six minutes!"

Dr. Maxwell looked at Ben as they rolled the woman into ER -1. "I don't know how much good we're doing, Ben, she's cyanotic. Even with help her heart's not doing what it's supposed to."

"We'll keep working her until you call it, Doc," panted the man working her chest. "You guys do what you have to do."

"Options?" Ben was looking at Dr. Maxwell, automatically deferring to the more experienced man.

"I have an idea," Maxwell said, turning from the dying woman and opening one of the many drawers in the ER. He withdrew a syringe, then reached into one of the voluminous pockets in his lab coat and drew forth a jar of a familiar milky liquid.

"What are you doing?" Ben's voice was a shocked hiss.

"Whatever I can," Maxwell said, snapping the lid off the jar and thrusting it into Ben's hands.

"Hold this."

"What? No!" Ben glanced at the center of the room where the team still worked.

Maxwell stripped the sterile cover from the syringe.

"It's perfect! According to the note this stuff is amazing for the heart."

"We don't know *what* that note says, remember? We don't even know what this *is*, never mind dosages, possible drug interactions—"

Maxwell thrust the tip of the syringe into the fluid and pulled back on the plunger, drawing some into the barrel. The smell of the stuff rose up to fill Ben's nostrils. It smelled like old gym socks tinged with meat gone bad and . . . something else. It smelled somehow *warm*, although that thought made no sense to Ben. Warm, and organic, and he turned his face away before he gagged. The old doctor gave no sign the smell even registered as he continued talking in hushed tones.

"Ben, this came from a country where they still slaughter chickens to ward off bad *ju-ju*. I don't think they're too concerned with precise dosages. As for everything else, well, look at it this way: She's dying. I can't make her any worse."

He raised the syringe and gave it a flick and squirt to get rid of any air bubbles trapped in the barrel. Their eyes locked, and Ben saw determination coupled with excitement in the old doc's eyes.

"Cap that," Maxwell said, pointing at the jar with his chin, "and keep it out of sight. If anything goes wrong I'll keep you out of it."

Without hesitation he turned and stepped to the gurney, chose his spot, and plunged the needle into the patient's arm. Ben screwed the cap on the jar, then put it in his pocket as they waited.

"Stop compressions," Maxwell commanded after 30 seconds. The paramedic stared at him, for a moment, then leaned back and gave his arms a rest, shaking out his hands. Maxwell looked only at the EKG readout. The woman's heart beat twice, nice and strong, then jittered. The beat became irregular, the heart racing.

"Tachycardia," reported the nurse.

"I can see that," snapped Maxwell. "Just wait."

The haywire rhythm continued for a few seconds, then leveled suddenly into one long flat note.

"She's crashing!" said the paramedic, already positioning his hands to resume CPR. The watching doctor barked an order.

"Wait!"

"But she's—"

"Just wait!"

Maxwell sounded commanding, his stance rigid and authoritative. Ben was the only one in the room who could see his hands locked behind his back, fingers twiddling nervously. As the seconds ticked by, Ben moved up to stand next to Dr. Maxwell. Though his eyes were on the girl who was gradually turning a lovely shade of blue, his ears caught the muttered words from the doctor next to him.

"Come on . . . come on . . ."

A nurse turned to Dr. Maxwell.

"Are you going to call time of death, Doctor?" Her voice was flat.

"I —" Maxwell began, but was interrupted by the EKG bursting into a rhythm again. No stuttering transition, no slow build; one moment that horrible flatline, the next a nice, steady beat.

"Yes!"

Maxwell gave a small, controlled fist pump of victory. The nurse got busy checking vitals as the EMT stepped down. They all watched the EKG bounce across the screen for almost a minute, waiting for it to falter again, but the beat remained strong and steady.

"Wow, Doc," said the paramedic. "Good call. I've never seen anything like that before. I thought she was gone."

The man gave an impressed snort, collected his partner, and walked out. Another nurse entered with an orderly in tow, the two of them preparing to move the patient to Recovery should she prove stable enough.

She did.

Maxwell ordered a battery of tests. To everyone else in the room he may have seemed merely thorough, but Ben knew what Maxwell was doing: searching for possible effects from the unknown drug with which he had injected the girl.

When Maxwell left ER-1 Ben followed, putting a hand on the older man's arm.

"That was risky as hell," he said. "What were you thinking, using that stuff?" He looked up and down the hall, making sure they were not overheard.

"Did you see that?" Maxwell's voice was filled with wonder.

"Yes," Ben said, "I saw it. I saw you using a drug that hasn't been tested or approved. Hell, we don't even know what it is!"

"But it worked!" Maxwell's eyes grew bright, almost manic. "It worked like a charm! Did you hear that man? 'Never seen anything like that before'!"

"Yes, I heard—" Ben began.

"This is just what we were looking for! It's . . . it's just what the doctor ordered!"

He grinned, oblivious to Ben's concern. He held out a hand.

"Give me the jar."

"What? No!" Ben was surprised, having forgotten he now carried the jar in his pocket.

Maxwell straightened, his voice commanding though he still spoke in low tones.

"Yes. Give it here. I need to draw up a few syringes so next time I won't be fumbling at the back of the room. That was almost a disaster."

"You can't keep using this stuff," Ben hissed. "It's not safe!"

Maxwell was calm. "I *can* keep using it, and I'll be on my own hook if I get caught."

His stare became icy, and Ben wondered just who this man was, this hard uncaring man who, just an hour earlier, had been his gentle mentor in this place.

"I'll be on my own *then*, but right *now* I have an accomplice."

Ben's own heart stuttered.

"What?"

"You knew what I was doing in there. You even helped fill the syringe, so you can't say you had no idea what was going on."

"But —"

"You knew—that makes you complicit. But I'm sure the disciplinary board will be lenient." Sarcasm filled his voice. "They are *so* known for leniency. And this is *exactly* the kind of thing a young doctor wants marking his career—supposing they even let you *have* a career, after all this!"

Ben's head was whirling with horror, and he felt nauseous. Maxwell smiled and extended his hand.

"Or, you can just hand me that jar right now and keep your mouth shut. It's really up to you, Ben. Your whole future is in your hands."

The grin dropped from his face. "Well? What's it going to be?"

Ben placed the jar in the waiting hand. Maxwell looked at the jar on his palm, his fingers curled around it, caressing the glass. He looked up at Ben, and his smile returned.

"Thanks, Ben. Toddle off now, and keep your mouth shut. Let me be all I can be!"

He strode off in the direction of his office, going to measure out some doses of his miracle cure. Ben watched until he turned a corner, then made his way back toward the center of the ER. He was moving slowly, in a daze.

He still felt like he was going to throw up.

***

BEN AVOIDED DR. MAXWELL for most of their shift together—quite a feat, considering he worked directly under the man. He kept his distance and tried to spot the old doctor using his miracle cure, but Maxwell was being cautious. Though he didn't catch him, Ben heard the glowing reports about Maxwell that night. Everywhere he went patients stabilized, even patients the other doctors labeled 'lost causes'. And not just heart cases.

Maxwell's shining moment came when they got word of a fifteen car pile-up on the freeway. The casualties were being brought to the closest trauma center: Springdale General. They had five minutes to prepare for the influx of patients, and Ben had to admit that Maxwell did an admiral job preparing the ER for a wave of nearly 30 new patients, all arriving within the span of a few minutes. He organized people and materials, implemented their Mass Casualty

Triage Plan, . . . then disappeared into his office for the last minute or so. Ben knew he was filling more syringes from his little jar of miracles, and any admiration he'd felt for Maxwell dissolved like a puff of bitter smoke.

Maxwell's plan worked just as he'd hoped; by the end of the shift he *was* walking around the ER as the hotshot doc. People were saying he'd saved at least half the patients from the pile-up himself. On his way out at the end of his 12 hour shift, Maxwell stopped by the nurse's station where Ben was using the phone to check on a patient who'd already been moved upstairs to recovery. Maxwell didn't say anything, just gave a wink and tipped his hat as he strolled toward the exit. Ben, working a double shift, barely spared him a glance as he pressed the receiver to his ear, trying to hear over the noise of the ER. He was checking on Rebecca Stillwell.

Rebecca Stillwell was their heart patient, the first to get a dose of what he'd begun to think of as 'Maxwell's Miracle'. The patient he himself had helped to dose with an unknown substance.

While Maxwell had run off to fill those first syringes, Ben had gone to the Admissions desk to collect Rebecca's information. Maxwell was listed as the attending physician, and Ben made certain it stayed that way. He signed nothing, just found out where Rebecca was being sent for recovery and started calling the nurse's station there. Self-preservation kept him 'officially' out of it, but his feelings of concern and guilt had him calling for status reports. The ER was busy, but he somehow managed a call every 30-45 minutes. Four hours into the recovery she was conscious. Six hours and she was up and about. He started to relax then, and slowed his calls to once an hour or so—good thing, too, since that was when they received the call about the freeway accident. Things got pretty busy after that.

Now, though, as Maxwell was skipping out the door, a nurse was telling Ben about Rebecca's sudden fever. There was no sign of infection, nothing that would have caused something like this. The increase in temperature registered only about 15 minutes before Ben's call, but had climbed from 100 to 102 in that time. The patient was in bed with a saline drip while they ran tests. Ben went cold, wondering just what the hell they had done to the girl. He asked to be kept apprised of her situation, then rang off to run beside another gurney, listening to an EMT reeling off case information. He immersed himself in the new case, focusing on the task at hand in an attempt to avoid wondering what he was going to do.

Unfortunately, 15 minutes later he was walking out of ER-2 with nothing to think about but his predicament.

*Maxwell used that stuff on quite a few patients without my aid, hell, without my **presence**. He's on the hook alone for all those . . . but I was there for Rebecca. I **did** hold the damn jar for him. It wasn't my fault, but Maxwell's been around forever. He knows people. He won't go down alone for this, I'm **sure** he'll take me —*

"Dr. Binder?"

Ben looked toward the nurse's station.

"Line one's for you. She has some patient info for you."

Ben scuttled over and grabbed the phone.

"Yes?"

"Dr. Binder? I'm calling about Rebecca Stillwell."

"Yes?"

"I'm sorry, Doctor. Her temp spiked to 106, so we started her in a cool bath. She coded while in the bath. The resuscitation team was called, but couldn't get her back. I'm sorry, Doctor, but she's already en route to the basement."

"What?" Ben checked the clock. "It hasn't even been 20 minutes since you told me about the fever *starting!*"

"I can't explain it, Doctor. Pathology will investigate, but at the moment we have no idea what went wrong."

I have an idea . . .

Ben hung up the phone, not realizing then that Rebecca was only the first.

All shift long Ben was fielding calls for Dr. Maxwell. Wherever his patients had been sent for recovery or tests, people were calling for him, wanting to know if there was anything they should know. Most of Maxwell's patients were exhibiting sudden and apparently sourceless fevers. These fevers spiked, and no matter what measures were taken resulted in death through cardiac arrest. Halfway through his shift these fevers exploded across the recovery ward, every one a victim in that freeway pile-up. That's when the math became simple.

12 hours! Ben thought. *12 hours after he injects them with that stuff, they're dead! It's the same every time!*

He phoned Maxwell again and again, but got no answer. He only hoped someone else in the hospital had better luck than he was having.

***

AT LAST HIS second shift ended. There had been an hour before dawn when everything seemed to quiet down, and it gave Ben time to think about Rebecca Stillwell, to wonder exactly what the hell had happened to her; to all of them. He felt guilt, but also, he had to admit, fear. Were they going to find out about Maxwell's potion? Chances were good. Would Maxwell absorb the blame and go down quietly, leaving Ben out of it as he'd said?

Not bloody likely.

He took his name off the "On Shift" board and hustled out of the ER. He was the picture of a man in a hurry to go home and get some sleep.

But he was going to the basement. To the morgue.

He knew he wasn't thinking straight. He'd been up for more than 24 hours; that was enough to make anyone a little fuzzy around the edges. He couldn't get the girl out of his mind—and he *had* held the jar . . .

He stumbled off the elevator into the visitor/viewing room, the room with the window where people came to identify the faces of loved ones. There, in the viewing room, was a woman.

He heard her before he saw her, the sounds of sobbing registering on his consciousness just before he associated the sound with the figure huddled in the chair next to the door leading into the morgue itself.

"Miss? Miss, are you all right?"

*Oh, **that's** a bright question to ask her **here**! She must have just identified—*

"Rebecca," the woman sobbed into her hands. "Rebecca's dead?"

The tone was disbelieving and mournful, and the words hit him like a slap.

"Rebecca? You mean Rebecca Stillwell?"

She looked at him though the mask of her fingers.

"Rebecca's dead."

"I know, I . . . we, uh—look, just wait here, I'll get Dr. Jonah, okay? Please."

He burst through the door into the morgue proper, mind whirling. "Dr. Jonah? Hello, Dr. Jonah?"

There were rows of refrigerated storage drawers, stainless steel handles gleaming under the cold fluorescents. There were gurneys, the door into the Autopsy Room, a desk and filing cabinet, but no sign of the pathologist. The door hissed behind him and Ben spun around, but instead of Dr. Jonah he found the woman following him. Standing, her face uncovered, she bore a striking resemblance to the girl Maxwell had injected with his potion almost a full day ago.

A sister?

"Miss? I'm sorry, but you shouldn't be in here."

As he moved to guide her back to her seat she reached toward him, and the grief etching her face nearly broke his heart.

"Rebecca's dead," she said again. "Help me, please?"

He caught her as she fell against him. Her dress was sleeveless, and as he touched her skin he was surprised at how cold she felt.

She must be in shock, he thought. *I'll have to get her to lie down. There must be a blanket somewhere—then I can call for assistance.*

"Come with me, all right? Sit down, please."

He put an arm about her shoulders to guide her, but she folded into his chest, her arms about him.

"Please, help me." Her words were muffled by his shirt, the scrubs so thin he could feel the chill of her cheek through the material. Ben moved them toward the closest seat, a nearby gurney, in a sort of shuffling dance.

"Let's sit you down for a minute, okay? Get you a blanket, all right?"

Her arms tightened about him, fingers splayed and caressing.

"Warm," she said, as if he had not spoken. "You're so warm. Oh my God. Help me."

"Now, I'm trying to—"

She kissed his neck.

He drew in a breath, shocked, but she didn't stop there. She continued to kiss down his neck to his throat as her hands caressed his back. She murmured into the hollow of his throat, her voice tickling his skin in a manner that had him standing on his toes.

"You're so warm, please help me . . . Rebecca's dead, and you're so warm . . ."

*Oh my God, this is just like that Forum in Penthouse last month, the one titled 'The Doctor is In'! I thought those stories were all bullshit! No! Wait—I have to get control of this, I can't **do** this!*

"Now, wait! Miss? No, I—look, Miss, we can't —"

But she was all over him, kissing and caressing, somehow peeling his scrub tunic upward to expose his skin, feeling his stomach, moaning about how warm he was, and how she needed his help. Her roving hand found the bulge at the front of his scrubs, squeezing and stroking, and Ben was lost. A minute later he was up on the gurney, flat on his back with his pants about his ankles as, dress pushed up to her hips, she swayed and bucked above him.

She rose and fell on him, around him, crushing him deeper into herself with every thrust, so hard it bordered on pain. Ben just tried to ride it out, to last long enough and not get hurt. Though she had started with kisses, all softness was gone from her. Her face was twisted into a rictus of need that was almost savage, and Ben realized he was not making love with a partner: he was being used to service her immediate need. Though that realization hurt a little, there was still a small part of him that thought *I have to write this down and send it in to Forums!*

He climaxed. There was nothing he could do to stop it, not thinking of baseball, going to his happy-place, nothing. It didn't slow her down in the least—he wasn't sure she even noticed. She pounded on him with increasing ferocity, her internal friction keeping him erect and functioning. He felt her teeth nipping and biting at his shoulders and throat. The combination of sharp little pains and her own frantic pleasure drove him over the edge again, his first ever double-orgasm. She stiffened, hands gripping the edges of the gurney to provide leverage, bearing down with more than just her weight as she ground herself onto him, harder and harder until he felt a final crushing squeeze deep within her, her release so strong it hurt, hurt a *lot*! The battering he'd just taken coupled with his 24 hour workday, and as he screamed at this sudden and unexpected pain, darkness closed over him.

He blacked out.

***

HE AWOKE TO a tickling near his groin, soft lips working their way down his hip. Eyes closed he moaned softly in anticipation. The kissing lips became softly nipping teeth as they worked their way down to his thigh . . . then an explosion of pain as they sank into his leg.

His eyes popped open and he stared down to find the girl gazing up at him, her teeth buried in his thigh to the gums. His scream, for he *was* screaming, increased in volume as she jerked her head upward, savagely twisting a huge chunk out of his leg. He rolled off the gurney, on the far side from where she was standing, the hole in his flesh spraying blood across the floor.

"Jesus *Christ!*"

She shoved the gurney, sending it flying out of the way. Ben scrambled away as she stumbled forward, bent over to grope for him clumsily as she chewed, then swallowed.

"What the hell are you doing!"

"Waaaaarrrmmmm . . . " she replied.

She batted his ankle in an attempt to grab. Ben scooted backward, his naked butt sliding easily over the blood-slicked floor. His feet were still tethered by his pushed-down pants, and somewhere he heard a banging noise. The girl was still staggering forward, eyes glassy, chin and chest covered with the blood from his leg like a child's bib gone horribly wrong.

He struggled to his feet, yanking up his pants despite the pain, slamming through the first doors he saw with a *swoosh.*

The autopsy theater.

He stumbled around the autopsy table, tripping over something on the floor. He caught the table edge and looked down.

Dr. Jonah, lying both face down and face up, his head twisted around 180 degrees, one eye missing, bite marks covering his face. Ben screamed as he heard the theater doors open, knowing it was the girl, but he couldn't take his eyes from Dr. Jonah.

The pathologist sat up. Ben saw the girl coming and backed away, saw her trip over Dr. Jonah, both of them going down in a heap. He lurched through the doors and back into the morgue. He grabbed the lamp from Dr. Jonah's desk and wound the cord through the handles to the autopsy room doors again and again. He backed away as, through the narrow inset windows he saw the girl, then the doctor, approach the doors. The bloodstained girl stared through the glass while Jonah shuffled over, head on backwards. The doors strained against the cord.

This can't be happening, he thought. *Jonah's dead, he* **has** *to be, and that girl . . . ohmigod, that's* **Rebecca** *isn't it? But . . . that means . . .*

His gorge rose as he recalled what had happened on that gurney, but he was distracted from those thoughts by the banging. The pounding. He followed the sound to the wall of cooler drawers. There were 30 small steel doors set into the wall, and fully 25 of them were moving. Jouncing. The steel handles shimmied, reflecting the lights.

More than 2 dozen . . . *things* were trying to get out.

Ben screamed, "What's going on?"

His mobile phone, lying on the floor by the gurney, began to chirp. He scrabbled for it, flipped it open.

"Hello?"

"Ben! Ben, my boy, where are you?"

It was Maxwell.

"Uh . . . still at the hospital, why?"

"I finally got in touch with Bill Harrison. Look, that stuff he sent me, it wasn't for use! It was something he . . . uh . . . *acquired* from some witch doctor there. Bill saw some remarkable things and sent me that sample for testing in a modern lab— I don't have time to go into that right now! I understand that girl we dosed with the stuff didn't make it?"

Emphasis on the *we*. Ben glanced at the face staring at him from the autopsy suite.

"Yeah, she's dead." His gorge rose again.

"Look, Ben, we have to do something. I'm driving, almost there. Meet me in the morgue in five minutes, got it? No excuses!"

"I'm way ahead of you, Doctor. I'll be waiting."

He closed the phone before Maxwell could reply. He looked down at his leg, still bleeding freely, and wiped a hand across his forehead. He was sweating profusely, the fever already upon him. His leg felt strange; a numbness that did not deaden the pain was radiating outward from the bite. His mind was foggy. He wondered how long he had, but decided it didn't matter.

He shuffled along yanking open doors and pulling out drawers.

Dr. Maxwell's patients rose up around him. As they tore into him he just hoped he'd have time to rise again before Maxwell arrived.

He did so want to greet the good doctor.

THE CHRYSANTHEMUM MOON

JACK IVEY

GUSTAV SAT PINING on an old log at the entrance to the long ago abandoned city park. His heart, though it did not beat, hurt immensely. Glancing up at the almost full moon he could only think that it had been their moon; their glowing orb of love hovering like a yellow chrysanthemum in the sky. He ripped off a finger and fastened it to a long branch with a few strands of his hair, using it to satisfy an itch in the middle of his back. There was a time, he thought, that this would not be necessary. She would have been happy to scratch the itch for him. But not anymore, the relationship was over and with it so was he. He could not live or not live without her in his undead life.

Gustav thought back to the first time he had set his eyes on her. He was in an alley over off of 4th Street, munching on a cocker spaniel he had cornered when she approached. He looked up with a mouth full of brown hair, spat it out and was shocked when it landed on top of her left foot. Reaching out to brush it free, he took a little of her skin with it. Raising his fingers to his nose, he could not help but notice her fragrance, as putrid and alluring as anything he had ever smelled before. She looked so hungry, with her beautiful grey eyes sunken into her head, Gustav invited her to join him. She wasted no time devouring the once family pet with the fervor of a fire ant mound that had been disturbed by some unsuspecting flesh. Gustav watched with enjoyment as every bone was stripped of its meat, as if she hadn't eaten in a month. He smiled so broadly that his lower jaw became momentarily dislodge from the upper. Seeing this she gently moved it back into position. Her touch was that of a rusted iron grate. He winced with delight as her scaly dirty fingers made contact with his face.

"I'm Gustav," he said with a wheeze and a hack. "I haven't seen you around here before." She backed a little into the corner, an expression very close to fear adorning her beautifully scarred and rotted face.

"Oh please, I will not hurt you. You sure seem to be hungry," offered Gustav in his most calming tone of cackle. Still, she said nothing but he could sense she was easing up a bit.

He told himself, no sharp moves. He didn't want to scare her off. "I hunt around here often. I'd know this place like the back of my hand if I still had the back of my hand."

He noticed a slight chuckle at his attempt at humor, but still no reply. "That's okay," he said. "If you don't want to talk I'm good with that. We can just sit here and relax a little, and then I will show you the best places to hunt if you'd like."

Gustav saw her looking up at the night sky; he turned his gaze as well. He saw a bright full moon glowing in the sky. After a few minutes of silence he said, "The moon sure is nice tonight."

She turned her attention back to him and this time she spoke in a whisper. "It is a very beautiful moon."

He loved the sound of her voice, like fingernails on a blackboard. It was like music to his ears as once again she went silent. "Yes, indeed it is beautiful," he answered trying to sound as intelligent as he could. "It looks as if it is a large yellow chrysanthemum blooming just for you."

She smiled at these words. He could see the lunar object's light reflecting on her scalp, and then watched as once again a smile made its way across the lower half of her face. They both sat there in the dark alleyway staring at the sky once again when she spoke.

"Ruth," she blurted out.

"I'm sorry?" he questioned.

"Ruth," she repeated herself. "You asked what my name is, it is Ruth."

He noticed she seemed to be becoming more comfortable with him. "That is a beautiful name. Pleased to meet you, Ruth," he responded.

"I am happy to meet you too, Gustav."

That night was the first night he had experienced the strange but real feeling: happiness. His life to that point had been filled with trying to satisfy his insatiable appetite for human flesh. Answering the call of his kind, searching endlessly for food, and watching as others around him fell to the weapons of the humans, never once caring about any of them. His only thoughts were of himself, which is why this had caught him so off guard. How could he possibly feel affection for another? It was not supposed to happen. But it did, and now nothing at all mattered to him. He picked up a stone and tossed it at nothing in particular.

A mouse scampered by; he reached out, grabbed it and swallowed it whole, without so much as a single chew. He felt it squirm within his stomach and wished it would stop; he was in no mood for fun of any kind. His heart was broken and ripped to shreds, which was normal, but the pain of his loss was not something he was used to. There was a good reason Zombies did not fall in love and this was it, he thought.

Still he could not get his mind off of her, off of Ruth. The nights they spent wandering the suburbs searching for unsuspecting humans to devour and the days they spent holed up in the basement of the old textile warehouse. Oh the warehouse, his nirvana, their place as it had become known to them. For the longest time it had just been a dark place for him to wait out the sun light, but she made it special. Her little touches made it feel so much like home. Once used only for sleeping now was their love palace, as strange as it seemed to him, this was where they made love. He felt a searing pain invade his gaping abdomen and it wasn't the mouse, it was the thought of never making love to her again.

It seemed so innocent at first, kissing and light petting; then that night she bit his lip—removing a piece of it, she swirled it about in her mouth. The look in her grey stoic eyes told him something magical was about to happen. It was then that he realized he had an erection and wasn't to sure what to do about it, but she was. As they lay naked on the cold damp concrete, she seductively scraped the scabs off of the inside of her vagina and allowed him to enter her. The sensation was amazing as they moved in perfect rhythm to each other until they both exploded in a simultaneous orgasm. He could not believe the feeling and wondered how he had gone so long without this before. He loved they way she looked as she lay there panting and used her fingers to bring about three more orgasms. Once she was finished he offered her a cigarette, but she declined, something about it being bad for her health.

Their lovemaking went on everyday when they would retire to the warehouse and he enjoyed every minute of it, but somehow it seemed to him it was becoming harder and harder to satisfy her; she wanted more. Though his erection constantly lasted more than four hours, he found himself reaching a climax long before she did.

The flash of headlights startled him from his self induced trance and he slithered into a nearby grove of bushes and waited for whoever it was to leave. Silently he watched as a group of armed humans scoured the area, searching for him and his kind. They were dangerously close when a radio in the car started to squawk: "Zombies spotted in the Chestnut Ridge area."

With that, the men quickly headed to their car and sped off into the night.

Gustav re-emerged from the bushes and made his way down to the edge of the large polluted lake and took a seat along its banks. He stared at the light of the moon reflecting off of the green stagnant water and thought, Ruth would have enjoyed this. She loved the moonlight and had taught him to enjoy its beauty. The shimmering ripples on the water danced about as his thoughts returned to the warehouse.

He asked her about this situation and what he might be doing wrong. He told her that he loved making love to her, but he realized he was not doing a good job of satisfying her and that was what was important to him. Ruth just brushed it off and replied to him that is was his satisfaction that was her main concern. But he would not let it rest, which he would find was the biggest mistake he would ever make. Once more they were engrossed in the throws of their lovemaking and he felt himself coming close to the end and he stopped and pulled out. Ruth looked at him with a concerned look and questioned, "Is there anything wrong?"

"Yes, there is. I feel like I am ready to explode and I sense you are no closer than you were when we started," he answered, in between the heavy breaths he was expelling.

"Oh Gustav, I told you that doesn't matter to me."

"Well it matters to me; tell me what I can do to bring you to orgasm?'

Ruth pulled him close, accidentally tearing a piece of skin from his shoulder and whispered in his ear something he had not expected: "Eat me."

"What?" he questioned as she spread her legs wide and rubbed her vagina with her fingers.

"Eat me Gustav, please eat me."

He watched as the gaping hole facing him was almost calling his name. Gustav was becoming more aroused then he could remember feeling in the past, his erection was rock hard and he felt sweat forming on his brow. He wasn't sure exactly what she wanted him to do, but she was almost begging him at this point, so he knew he had to do something.

He dove in head first and was amazed by her loud and sensuous moans. As he moved his mouth about her body, her moans quickly became screams and he lost all control of himself. He loved the way she tasted and her screams were arousing him even more than he thought possible. Her fingernails dug deep into his back and he continued to work his mouth in ways he still did not understand. Before he knew it she was writhing, arching her back and screaming the loudest scream he had every heard and as quickly as she had started, Ruth was quiet. He was aghast at what he had done, before him lie only the skeletal remains of the woman he had fallen madly in love with.

He cried as he pleaded to the unresponsive skeleton, "Why did you ask me to eat you, why oh why would you beg something of that from me?"

Gustav stared off into the dark green abyss sitting peacefully in front of him; his world shattered and nothing remained, at least nothing that mattered to him. Once again he saw the glare of lights heading in his direction, only this time he did not hide. He stood and faced the group of men now approaching him. He watched as they shone their lights on him and one raised his weapon. He listened as a shot was pulled off and winced as the bullet expertly found his tiny brain, blowing it to bits. His lifeless body fell into the water and floated out, now surrounded by the glow of the moon, the glow of their chrysanthemum moon.

There was a good reason zombies did not fall in love, and this was it.

LOVE NEVER DIES

TAWN KRAKOWKSI

HE SHUFFLED AIMLESSLY near the structure in the near pitch darkness. Ambling with his crooked, hitching gait, he knew *she* was inside. He ached for her. Hungered, like a man deprived of air. He also knew that she would have to come out eventually, and when she did, they would be together ... forever.

***

THOMAS WAS RIDING a bicycle he had found abandoned in an alley when he came across the building. He was on his way to check on extended family that had been living in Wisconsin. He didn't really expect to find them, but the journey was all he really had left after his wife and three children had been turned. He didn't have it in him to kill them—even as a mercy—so instead, he ran. Like the lowliest coward, he left them to whatever existence they had left. Not a day went by that he didn't think about what he had done and how much he had lost. But if he had to do it all over again, he knew he would choose the same horrific path, despite the fact that it led straight into the bowels of Hell.

A large "911" printed on the front of the structure above the door declared it to be an emergency center. Thomas had been an electrician before the virus had mercilessly swept through this part of Illinois. Many people hadn't known of the treasure trove of electronics, emergency supplies, and security benefits that such a place boasted or even where to find them. This meant that most emergency centers were relatively intact, even after all the Walmarts everywhere had been looted into oblivion. He approached the building warily, circling completely around it twice to verify as best he could that it hadn't been compromised, and then went to work on getting the door open. He had to hurry. It would be nightfall soon.

To his vast surprise, it clicked open before he even had a chance to decide the best way to force the lock. Thomas heard a woman's voice beckon him inside, further adding to his confusion. Since zombies don't do much more than snarl, grunt, and bite, he figured it was safe to enter. Once past the front door, he found himself in a short, dimly lit corridor designed to be very much like an airlock on a submarine. The metal door at the far end of the hallway could not be opened until the outer door had been closed and whomever was inside pressing the buttons decided the visitor was welcome.

What if this is some sort of trap? Thomas suddenly wondered, as apprehension crawled up his spine. Only when he heard the click of the inner door did relief drown his irrational fear. Thomas pushed through the second security door and was greeted by a slightly plump yet still athletic-looking woman with short mousy-brown hair and a vacant look in her hazel eyes. There was nothing extraordinary about her looks, but the way she carried herself and the tone of her voice identified her as someone teetering on the razor edge of despair.

"My name is Sandra," she said tonelessly, before turning her back to him to lead him further into the facility. The center was built like a bunker. Before the apocalypse—that's what those who were still human called it—the structure was used as a police station in addition to an emergency response center and was well fortified against attacks from the outside.

Thomas was surprised to find that it was also well provisioned within. The first room she led him through had been an office and was set up as a first line of defense with several riot shotguns, 9mm automatic handguns, boxes of ammunition, and even the sleek black clubs with handles that were issued to cops. There were flashlights, boxes of batteries, and even a couple of outfits Thomas assumed were standard issue riot gear. A team of navy seals couldn't get past this room without divine intervention, even if the only defender was a child.

"How long have you been here, Sandra?" Thomas asked, marveling at the arsenal.

"Three months. My husband was a dispatcher here ... before ..." She abruptly shoved the knuckle of her right index finger into her mouth and bit down hard to stifle the tears already threatening to spill onto her pale cheeks.

Thomas didn't need to hear any more to know what had happened. Her husband had been bitten and turned. Just like his own family.

"My name is Thomas," he said, introducing himself to combat the awkward silence that had developed between them, as each mournfully remembered what they had lost.

"Welcome to Hell, Thomas," she replied so softly that he missed it.

***

SANDRA SHOWED THE tall, gaunt man she had let into the facility where the supplies had been stashed. In addition to all of the guns in the front office, she and Reggie had loaded three of the four cells in the basement with provisions. One cell was their pantry, loaded top to bottom with canned food. A second cell held water. They had been able to obtain six racks each holding eighteen full five-gallon jugs of bottled water, which they had used and refilled in the early days when the water supply had still been uncontaminated and fresh from the taps. Now she had just over four racks full of water left and no way to refill them with untainted water. Even boiling the gunk that came out of the faucets could not make it drinkable.

The third cell held cans of gasoline for the large generator located upstairs that was jury-rigged to direct its exhaust outside, propane tanks for cooking when the gas company was no longer supplying gas—which came to pass only two weeks ago—and all the lighters, kitchen matches, and butane refills they could find on all of their pre-apocalyptic scouting missions. There was even a pile of homemade torches for when the generator could no longer provide light.

"And this last cell is the sleeping quarters." Her voice broke from the heartbreak that had not faded in the last three months. The man— *Thomas,* she reminded herself—took her into his arms, hesitantly at first, but it wasn't long before he was sobbing as desolately as she was. Sandra's grief was so raw, so bottomless that he was swept away by her emotional maelstrom. They stood, clinging to each other, weeping, until Sandra emptied her broken soul and her breath came in ragged gasps.

Oh, Reggie...

***

THE DECREPIT, SHAMBLING creature that used to be Reggie was so far gone now that he couldn't even remember her name. Or his own. But the miniscule part of him that was still alive, that remained locked away deep inside, imprisoned by the catastrophe that had transformed him into an animated corpse, that part knew her. Loved her. But that was the extent of his awareness. He only knew that she was his reason for being. In some primitive way, perhaps he sensed that she could free him from his abhorrent captivity so he would no longer be forced to commit the most heinous of crimes to feed the cravings within his rotting dungeon. If she could love him again, as she had before he had become this...*thing*...then maybe he could finally be at peace.

***

THOMAS AWKWARDLY RELEASED the despondent woman from his arms and wiped his own eyes. Somehow, her raw pain had blown apart the barrier that he had erected around his emotions as if it were nothing more sturdy than a house of cards. Comforting her had initially made him feel a bit better, reaffirming his place among humanity after his vile abandonment of his loved ones. Now, however, something felt wrong. As if she were feeding on his pain, sucking him dry. He feared that soon nothing would be left but a husk if he did not push her away.

"I'm sorry," Sandra sulked. She didn't even bother to dry her tears, allowing them to glisten and dissipate on her cheeks. "It's been so long with only my nightmare for company. I just ... couldn't ..."

Thomas interrupted her confession. "Your nightmare? What do you mean?"

"I'll show you," she replied. "Come look at the monitor."

Intrigued, Thomas followed her back up the stairs to the main floor. Sandra led him into a room which contained four high tech computer workstations. This must have been where the 911 dispatchers had worked before the world was turned upside down.

To conserve energy, Sandra had a single station operational with only one monitor on. She turned to Thomas and said, "Tell me what you see on the monitor."

Thomas tilted his head quizzically at her before honoring the request. The screen cycled through the images piped in from various cameras located around the facility. "What the..." Thomas breathed as he saw a shadow, darker than the surrounding night, clumsily trudge past the door from which he had entered not so long ago.

"I let you in because I couldn't stand to watch him...*it*...kill another one," she shuddered in horror.

"*Another* one?" Thomas' creeping apprehension returned, running its icy fingers lazily from his neck to the base of his spine. "You mean it comes here to feed or something? But they don't do that. They wander around and kill whatever they come across. They don't *hunt!*"

"He never leaves," Sandra whispered hauntingly and moved deeper into the room to Thomas' right.

Thomas found the control inputs for the cameras and removed all the other feeds from the cycle so that he could more closely watch Sandra's zombie. He said nothing as he concentrated, brow furrowed, for another ten minutes on the image shown on the monitor. "It's still out there," Thomas said, nodding at the camera. "I can't figure it out. What does it want?"

"Me," Sandra said without looking at him.

She sat on a desk in the abandoned 911 center, hugging herself tightly. She had been terrified and sad for so long now that her overwrought emotions, agitated when Thomas had held her, had morphed into a detached hollowness. She didn't have to see Reggie on the monitor to know that he was waiting for her. But the thing that waited outside was no longer the man that she had loved with wild abandon. It was a hollow shell that was all that remained of the Reggie who had succumbed to the last wave of the virus that had nearly scoured mankind from the planet.

A rotting corpse which had, until three months ago, been her husband.

"You?" Thomas' voice cut through her misery. "What are you talking about?"

"It was my husband, Reggie," Sandra told him. "He was turned three months ago and hasn't left."

Thomas was so baffled that he could not process what Sandra had told him. "He hasn't left? That zombie has just been hanging around for *three months*?!"

"*DON'T CALL HIM THAT!*" Sandra screeched, her hazel eyes erupting into a wildfire of anger fueled by anguish and fear. Her voice pitched higher as her denials became more vehement. "He's not a zombie! He's NOT!" She clutched at her short hair, whipped her head from side to side, and repudiated all of Thomas' startled attempts to soothe her before she streaked toward the front door without warning.

Thomas' utter shock kept him rooted in place for a moment too long. He sprinted into the office that was outfitted like NRA headquarters just as the inner door banged closed.

"NO! Oh, God, NO!" Thomas prayed to a God he no longer believed in that he would find the button to seal her into the corridor before she could do the unthinkable. He searched frantically around the room, but the hollow sound of the outer door opening stabbed at his heart an instant before he found the control panel.

Sandra was already outside.

***

THE MONSTER THAT stalked the building in the dark night halted its lonely rounds, sensing that something had changed. A loud noise and *her* sweet voice echoing into the parking lot heralded the end of his suffering. She had come. At last, she would save him and his hunger would be quenched.

***

SANDRA HAD COME entirely undone. The frayed bits of her mind that she had thought to mend by letting a stranger into her sanctuary had been the very thing to finally break her. She had heard the man she had saved from the *thing* outside use that disgusting

Love Never Dies | **135**

word to describe Reggie, her soul mate. But it just couldn't be true. Reggie was not a monster. Reggie loved her. He couldn't...*wouldn't*...

She had to know. She had to find out the truth...whether or not even the most miniscule speck of what had filled her heart with so much love remained. Why else would he still be here, but for her? Maybe he needed her help. Sandra could not hide in her fortress anymore. She had to be with Reggie even if there was nothing left of the man she loved.

***

THOMAS RAN BACK the way he had come to the dispatcher workstation. He didn't want to watch the broken woman be torn to bits by her zombie husband, but the guilt that this was somehow his doing needed to be assuaged. Sandra had to be delusional, insane. Zombies simply did not behave in the manner she insisted this one did.

Thomas watched the monitor, frozen in horror as the woman and the zombie closed the distance between them, like a cheesy movie where lovers run to each other through a field of blooms in slow motion. He hoped against hope that her death would be quick and painless, that she wouldn't be turned instead. *Maybe that's what she wants*, materialized unbidden in Thomas' mind.

He squeezed his eyes shut and clenched his jaw in an effort to force the repulsive thought from his head. When he opened his eyes and focused again on the image on the monitor, he saw the plump, short-haired woman with the tear-stained cheeks fall into the arms of the ravenous walking corpse. The scream Thomas fully expected to hear despite the lack of speakers did not come. The awful sounds of the rending of flesh and warm blood splashing on the concrete played only in Thomas' imagination. Against everything Thomas knew to be true, Sandra—still alive and unbitten—was snuggled in the putrid arms of her zombie lover.

Thomas' appalled disbelief overpowered his rising need to be sick and he absently swallowed the bile in the back of his throat. He sat down heavily in the rolling office chair at the desk, still staring aghast at the monitor. *If that zombie was still human enough to remember Sandra, then what hellish nightmare must my wife and children be experiencing? Can love really overcome a zombie's hunger? Oh, God, what have I done?*

Thomas buried his face in his hands and wept bitterly a second time in less than a day. He didn't need to see the woman and her zombie wander hand in hand into the night to know in his heart that he had just witnessed proof of the power of love.

Jake Cesarone (aka, Chicago Jake) is a part-time writer of genre fiction including Science Fiction, Mystery, Fantasy, and Horror. In real life, he is a mild-mannered Engineering Professor at a small school in Chicago, but by night, he sits down at his 1908 Underwood #3 and bangs out pages and pages of portentous prose and pretentious pabulum. He enjoys photography, architecture, movies, gangsters, and ghosts. Although fond of travel, there are several Caribbean countries which he can no longer visit, due to a price on his head.

Jack Ivey is an accomplished musician and songwriter whose talent leans toward the poetic variety. His creative writing accomplishments include several poems published in Dark Eclipse and over 100 Flash Fiction stories published on Helium.com. His family keeps him grounded while his imagination sets him free. A native of New Jersey, he moved to South Texas via a Trailways bus 35 years ago and has called this region home ever since.

Born and raised in Illinois yet inexplicably filled with Aloha Spirit, **Tawn Krakowski** is a wife, mother, pilot, entrepreneur, writer and an almost insufferable optimist. Tawn has a Bachelor of Science degree in Aviation Management, and has worked as a both a cargo and charter jet pilot before turning her family's life upside down by investing in a Maui Wowi Hawaiian Coffees & Smoothies business, which she operates in conjunction with her writing and voice-over projects. A voracious reader from an early age, Tawn is a sucker for horror, science fiction, and fantasy, although the she is always on the prowl for anything new and exciting. Her serial fiction, Darkling Drake and The Pirate Princess are available in both written and audio format at BigWorldNetwork.com, and you can peruse her blog at TotallyTawn.wordpress.com . Tawn is also seriously addicted to Facebook, so please feel free to like, comment, share, subscribe, fan, friend and otherwise cyberstalk her at Facebook.com/TawnKrakowski.

Christopher Law lives in Dover, UK. "The Shelter" is his first published story; be on the lookout for his contribution to the anthology, 'GUN'. He is currently working on a novel called 'Gorgeous'.

Araminta Star Matthews has a terminal degree in creative writing and works in higher education as an instructional designer serving the University of Maine System. Her young-adult, zombie apocalypse novel, Blind Hunger, was released by Dark Moon Books in 2011 and is available at various booksellers online. She also co-authored Write of the Living Dead, a cross-genre writing manual narrated by a cast of undead characters, in an effort to address the concerns of writing teachers and students grappling with stale writing guides as textbooks. That title was released by Dark Moon Books in 2012. She has several shorter works appearing in anthologies, such as Slices of Flesh and Trans-Kin, and she freelances for various magazines. She is currently coauthoring a young-adult zombedy ("zombie-comedy") with Stan Swanson, and has plans for a collaborative work with Max Booth III. She lives in Central Maine with her life partner, Abner, and their energetic whippet, Devo.

Bruce Memblatt is a native New Yorker, and a member of the Horror Writers Association. He is on the staff of The Horror Zine as Kindle Coordinator. His story "Dikon's Light" is a recipient of Bewildering Stories 2012 Mariner Awards. His works have been published over one hundred times in antholgy books, magazines and zines such as Aphelion, Post Mortem Press, Dark Moon Books, Sam's Dot Publishing, Strange Weird and Wonderful Magazine, The Horror Zine, Midwest Literary Magazine, Danse Macabre, Parsec Ink, The Feathertale Review, Yellow Mama and many more.

Kevin McClintock, who hails from Joplin, Missouri, has published 31 stories in the past two years, and has appeared in a number of horror magazines and anthologies. His collection of stories, "No Vacancies," was published in 2011 by Dark Moon Books.

Jessica McHugh is an author of speculative fiction that spans the genre from horror and alternate history to epic fantasy. A prolific writer, she has devoted herself to novels, short stories, poetry, and playwriting. She has had twelve books published in four years, including the bestselling "Rabbits in the Garden," "The Sky: The World" and the gritty coming-of-age thriller, "PINS." More info on Jessica's speculations and publications can be found at JessicaMcHughBooks.com.

Benjamin More writes science fiction and horror stories. Fiction has become a tolerable outlet for his incessant lying, or as he calls it, storytelling. Peculiar inquiries and absurd experiences spawn bacterial strains of unnatural adventures which have become the reason resistant cultures of his craft. He resides in the zombie capital of the world, Riverside California, with his lovely wife and two small children. Fortunately for the universe his family keeps him grounded. Otherwise he might get lost in space or dive brains-first into the zombie apocalypse. For more visit Benjaminmore.wordpress.com.

Rob Mosca is a freelance zombie apocalypse survival coach in Atlanta, Georgia. Or at least that's what he fills out on his unemployment benefit forms. However, until society crumbles under the relentless waves of flesh ravenous undead, he makes a little walking around money as the author of delightfully visceral and absurd tales. His debut novel, High Midnight, is a ghoul infested love letter to spaghetti westerns and pulp adventure magazines. It's currently available from Dark Moon Books... or at least will be until there's no more room in Hell and the dead begin walking the earth.

Kurt Reichenbaugh lives in Phoenix where he spends his daylight hours trying to convince his doppelganger to blow the corporate gig once and for all, and follow his passions into a happy, fulfilled, semi-obscurity. Until then, he is content to write, edit and collect vintage paperpacks with covers of semi-clad babes and laconic men. His stories can be found in several small press projects. His novel SIRENS will be published by PMMP in 2013. His mom thinks he's the best thing since sliced bread and microwave ovens. His girlfriend isn't sure. You can follow his blog at theringerfiles.blogspot.com.

Rob Smales spends his days delivering mail in a small New England town, and his nights writing Things Dark and Scary. And happy little Christmas stories. But mostly Things Dark and Scary. You can find out more about him at his website at www.RobSmales.Webs.Com, where he releases weekly flash Horror fiction, or contact him directly at Robert.T.Smales@Gmail.Com. Or you can find him lurking in the background at various book sales, conventions and readings around New England. Yup. Lurking.

Jay Wilburn lives in beautiful Conway, South Carolina with his wife and two sons. His novel Loose Ends: A Zombie Novel is available now. His next novel Time Eaters will be released in November of 2013. He has published numerous horror and speculative fiction stories. Follow his many dark thoughts at JayWilburn.com or @AmongTheZombies on Twitter.

Jennifer Word is an award-winning poet and editor in Southern California. She holds a B.A. in Psychology from Pepperdine University. Her Science & Speculative Fiction trilogy series *The Society, Book One: Genesis* is now available c/o Stony Meadow Publishing, and can be purchased at Amazon and Barnes & Noble online. Her short fiction and poetry has been featured in *The Storyteller Magazine, The Klondike Sun, Dark Moon Digest, Dark Eclipse e-Magazine, Surreal Grotesque Magazine, eFiction Magazine*, and the *Frightmares* and *Slices of Flesh* anthologies, as well as *From Beyond the Grave*, published by Grinning Skull Press.. She is also the author of *"The Poe Toaster," "All Because of the Cat"*, and *"Higher Love"*, available on Amazon and in the Smashwords Premium Catalog as e-books. Her website: www.fictionspook.com . Her debut horror e-novella, *RAIN*, is now available from Dark Moon Books and can be purchased for the Nook and Kindle at Amazon.com and Barnes&Noble.com.